I0722019

# HAILEY'S HAVEN

---

## SMOKY MOUNTAIN SECRETS

LAURA SCOTT

Copyright © 2020 by Laura Iding

All rights reserved.

No part of this book may be reproduced in any form or by any electronic or mechanical means, including information storage and retrieval systems, without written permission from the author, except for the use of brief quotations in a book review.

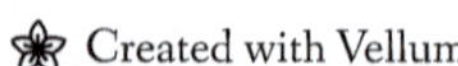 Created with Vellum

Hailey Donovan gently patted the donkey with sympathy. "I'm sorry, Rory. Next time I'll move faster to save you from being hurt." Rory brayed loudly and kicked out with his left back hoof. The donkey was just one of the many farm animals living on the Rhodes Hobby Farm, and as ornery as he was, Rory was one of her favorites. Lucy, the spitting baby llama, was a close second.

The June Tennessee sun was brutal, and rivulets of sweat dripped down her back. Despite the heat and tourism of the summer, she preferred working outdoors rather than being cooped up in an office building.

Yeah, she'd tried that once. It didn't go well.

The Smoky Mountains loomed high behind her, and she took a few steps toward the towering trees that offered shade. Hailey's boss, Nora Rhodes, was making sure the kids were safely tucked on their school bus. Hailey appreciated Nora giving her a job five years ago, despite her checkered past. Now they functioned more like partners than boss and employee.

"Any problems?" Nora asked, coming over to join her.

"Just that one little boy, Owen, who kept pinching Rory." She shook her head. "He's lucky he didn't get hurt by one of Rory's vicious kicks."

"Kids." Nora huffed. "They never learn. We're finished for the day. You should head home. We have another busload of kids coming again tomorrow."

"I know." Without the bus tours, Hailey wouldn't have a job, but it was still difficult to drum up enthusiasm for a repeat of today's events. "Do you want me to help with the rest of the livestock first?"

"I've got it." Nora waved a hand. "You've been here since six thirty, and it's past four. I'll see you in the morning."

"Okay." Hailey gratefully nodded and slipped past Nora toward the back of the farm where her rusty Chevy truck was parked. The small mobile home she rented on a month-to-month basis was several miles away but within walking distance of her favorite hiking trail.

Her trailer was small and plain, but it offered a roof over her head, which she considered a luxury. It didn't take long for her to switch out her work boots for hiking shoes, grab a refillable water bottle from her fridge, and head up the trail. Within minutes, the stress of the day faded away.

She went about two miles before cresting at the top of a hill overlooking the Grassy Branch of Little Pigeon River. After drinking from her water bottle, she lifted her gaze to the eagle soaring overhead. Hailey caught her breath at the magnificent sight, loving the glimpses of wildlife teeming in the forest.

A rock beneath her right heel slid, sending her off balance. As she caught herself on a scrubby bush, a sharp report rang out.

Instinctively, she dropped to the ground near the scrub

brush. Her water bottle hit the dirt and rolled off the edge of the trail, falling into the valley below. She barely noticed. There was no hunting allowed in the Smoky Mountain National Park, so it was confusing to hear what sounded like gunfire.

A second shot rang out, and a bit of dirt punched up from the ground less than six inches from her face.

*Someone was shooting at her!*

Hailey scrabbled backward, seeking more coverage, which wasn't easy on the narrow hiking trail. Avoiding the steep drop where her water bottle had disappeared, she did her best to find a hiding spot behind a grouping of large trees.

Her breathing hitched in her chest as she strained to listen above the hammering of her heart. No way to tell where the gunfire had come from. She eased deeper into the foliage, being careful not to rustle any leaves or step on any twigs. Months of hiding in the wilderness served her well. She knew how to blend in.

For several long moments, there was nothing but silence. Still, she didn't move. Patience was her friend, and she'd stay out here until darkness had fallen if necessary.

Yet it didn't make any sense that someone wanted to hurt her. Not after all this time. Maybe thirteen years ago, after she and the rest of the foster kids had escaped the Preacher's cabin.

But not now. Not after the cabin of horrors had been burned to the ground. The Preacher and his wife, Ruth, had died that day, and while she felt certain his demise hadn't been intentional, she couldn't find much sympathy for the man who'd made her life, and those of the other foster kids in his care, a living terror.

Footsteps pounded on the trail. She froze, not even

daring to breathe. Peering between the leaves, she watched the open spot of the trail, expecting to see someone with a gun searching for her.

Although if he was trying to hide, the pounding footsteps were a dead giveaway.

When a tall, broad-shouldered man emerged in her line of sight, she was surprised to see he was indeed carrying a gun. A handgun, not a rifle. And he was dressed in the tan and green uniform of the DNR Park Rangers, complete with the wide-brimmed hat shadowing his face.

The shooter? She didn't think so. Not that she trusted a man wearing a uniform, because she didn't. But that distrust didn't make the ranger a bad guy. She was fairly certain the gunfire had come from a rifle. Not a handgun.

The ranger stopped directly in her line of vision and spoke into his radio. "The trail is clear, no sign of the shooter or the woman that was hit."

It took her a minute to realize the ranger thought she'd been injured by the gunfire. He must have had eyes on her when she'd dropped to the ground at the same time the shot rang out. It was tempting to come out of the trees, but years of experience hiding from the law had her hanging back.

The ranger crouched down, staring intently at the exact spot on the trail where she'd gone down. Her heart began to pound as she realized he would easily be able to follow the tracks she'd left behind, marring the dirt in her haste to seek cover.

Taking control of her own destiny, Hailey abruptly stood and emerged from her hiding spot. The ranger shot up to his feet, leveling his gun at her for a fraction of a second before lowering it again.

"Are you hit?" He raked his keen gaze over her, his deep husky voice catching her off guard.

"No." She didn't dare take her eyes off him. "Do you have any idea which direction the shots came from?"

"The northeast." He returned her stare with one of his own, then reached for his collar. "I found her, she's not hurt. Repeat, female hiker is not injured."

"Ten-four," the voice on the radio squawked in reply.

The name tag over his left breast pocket indicated his last name was Wilson, no clue what his first name was. He was about her age, maybe a little older. It was hard to tell because his face was weathered by the sun, much the way hers was.

"Any idea why someone might be shooting at you?" Ranger Wilson asked.

"No." She glanced around the area, realizing that walking back down the trail to where her trailer house was located would be heading straight toward the shooter if Wilson was right about the direction the shots had come from. Well okay, then. No reason not to keep hiking the trail for a while longer. She turned away and began walking.

"Hey, where are you going?" Ranger Wilson's deep voice was rough with irritation. "I need to talk to you."

Hailey suppressed a sigh and turned back to face him. "About what?"

His gaze beneath the brim of his hat narrowed. "About the gunfire that was clearly meant for you. What's your name?"

Her gut clenched as her past dealings with law enforcement flashed in her mind. Logically, she knew she couldn't be in trouble, but old habits were hard to break. She forced the words out of her tight throat. "Hailey Donovan."

"Where do you live, Ms. Donovan?"

Her chin lifted a notch. "In the Whispering Oaks Trailer Park."

If he thought that made her some sort of lowlife, he didn't let on. "Where do you work?"

She hesitated, wondering why any of this mattered. "I work for Nora Rhodes at the Rhodes Hobby Farm."

He nodded, presumably familiar with the local tourist attraction. "Okay, Ms. Donovan, I'm going to ask you again. Are you absolutely sure you don't know of anyone who might be holding a grudge against you? An old boyfriend? Husband? Anyone?"

"I already told you, I don't know anyone who would do this. The last boyfriend I had, Jacob, left me for someone else, so I doubt he'd come back to shoot at me with a gun. And I've never been married." She felt her temper slipping a bit. "The only person I yelled at today was a seven-year-old named Owen who kept pinching Rory our donkey. That's about as exciting as my life gets."

The corner of his mouth twitched in a half smile. "Pinching a donkey, huh? Not very smart. I'm surprised he didn't get kicked."

"No kidding." She crossed her arms over her chest. "Frankly, he would have deserved it, but I hauled him out of harm's way. I also yelled at him, told him to keep his pinching fingers to himself. I don't take kindly to animal abuse in any way, shape, or form." In Hailey's opinion, animals were far better companions than people.

His quirky smile faded. "Me either. Okay, Ms. Donovan. I'll escort you home."

Uh-uh. No way. "I'm not going home. I'm heading up the trail. I'm sure that guy was poaching or something. Whatever he was doing doesn't involve me." As she turned away, Ranger Wilson's hand shot out with surprising quickness to grab her arm.

"No, you aren't going up the trail." His tone was even,

but there was no mistaking the underlying layer of steel. "You don't know what the shooter was up to, and neither do I. We'll investigate from our end and keep our eyes out for anything suspicious. In the meantime, it's my job to keep you safe. We're going back down the mountain."

She wanted to dig in her heels but had to consider the fact that doing so would only make him more curious about her. The last thing she wanted was for the ranger to know about the stint she'd done in juvie. The incident had been a little over ten years ago, but that didn't matter in the so-called justice system.

"Fine." She glanced back up at the sky. The bald eagle was long gone. Disappointed, she turned and moved past the ranger.

Another shot rang out. Ranger Wilson reacted quickly, pulling her down to the ground and covering her body with his. Her head hit something hard, making her wince. There was a thud, and she heard him mutter something harsh.

"What's wrong?" she whispered.

"Lost the radio." His voice was right next to her ear. "We're moving into the trees, got it?"

"Yes." She wanted to point out that hiding in the trees was exactly what she'd done the first time she'd heard gunfire but decided he wouldn't appreciate it. Especially since she must have been the one who'd knocked his radio loose.

Moving swiftly, he levered up, placing himself in front of her so she could crawl on her hands and knees to the forest. Surrounded by trees made her feel safe.

But the third gunshot, especially while she was next to a ranger, was disturbing. Apparently, Wilson was right.

She was a target. Someone wanted to kill her. But who?

And more importantly, why?

ROCK WILSON COULDN'T BELIEVE he'd lost his radio over the edge of the cliff. He still had his cell phone, but coverage was sparse in the Smoky Mountains.

Hidden in the trees along the edge of the trail, he thought about the gunfire. That third shot had been reckless considering he'd been standing right next to Hailey Donovan. Most people, especially poachers, didn't shoot at park rangers.

So why had the shooter taken the risk? No clue.

He glanced at Hailey. She was crouched beside him and appeared far too calm for someone who had been shot at three times.

She was roughly five feet five inches tall and lean, with long straight dark hair that she pulled back from her face in a ponytail. Her clothing was plain—a green T-shirt, blue jeans, and a green baseball cap. He found himself wondering if she'd worn the green on purpose, to blend into the foliage around them.

He estimated her age to be in her midtwenties, give or take a year, likely younger than his twenty-nine. There was no doubt in his mind she knew more than what she'd revealed. He was determined to hear the complete story, but for now, they needed to find a safe place to hide from the shooter.

Preferably somewhere his cell phone might work to call for backup.

Hailey didn't move for several minutes, and he had to admire her patience. Most women he knew wouldn't have been able to remain so still. She was clearly at home in the wilderness, and he found himself curious about her background.

Long minutes passed without either one of them breaking the silence. He finally leaned close, speaking in a low voice. "You were right the first time. We need to change course and head up the mountain, staying hidden in the trees."

She nodded in agreement. Again, he was impressed with her ability to immerse herself in nature.

He went first, doing his best not to broadcast their position. Initially, he feared Hailey would disappear on him, but she didn't. She remained behind him, moving stealthily through the brush.

After roughly twenty minutes, he stopped at a large boulder that looked as if it had been dropped from the sky to land in the middle of the forest. Using a stick, he swept around the base of the rock searching for snakes. There were dozens of snakes in the mountains, but only two poisonous ones, the northern copperhead and the timber rattler. A harmless grass snake slithered away, disappearing into the brush.

Rock lowered himself to the ground and leaned against the boulder. Hailey dropped down too, leaving a three-foot gap between them.

He pulled his canteen off his belt and offered it to her.

With a moment's hesitation, she accepted the canteen but took only a very small sip of water before handing it back. "Thanks."

He took a small sip, too, then capped the canteen to preserve what was left. He wasn't sure how long they'd be out here, but it was better to be on the safe side and conserve what they had. He pulled out his cell phone and held it up in an attempt to find a signal. No bars. He sighed and tucked it back into his pocket. "There's an abandoned cabin not far from here, we could hole up there for a while."

She stiffened and glanced at him. "There's no reason to hide out in a cabin. We can make a wide circle and still find a way down to the road while staying hidden in the forest."

"We could," he agreed. "But what if someone is down there waiting for you?"

"I'm sure there's not."

He lifted a brow. "Enough to bet your life on it?"

She glanced away, staring off into the distance for a long moment. "I don't understand what's going on. There is absolutely no reason for anyone to shoot at me. I work at a hobby farm. Nothing dangerous about that."

He nodded. "It's curious someone took a shot at you while standing next to a ranger. He must know the entire team will be scouring the mountains looking for him."

She shrugged. "Yeah, but how many rangers are there? Not nearly enough to cover the entire area."

It was a good point. "We might be able to get a cell signal at the abandoned cabin." At least he hoped so.

Hailey scowled, not happy with the plan, but she didn't argue. He took her silence as agreement. After resting for another five minutes, he rose to his feet. "Ready?"

Without saying a word, she reluctantly joined him.

He'd never spent so much time with a woman who didn't ramble on about unimportant stuff. Her comfort at being in the wilderness and her ability to remain still and silent intrigued him. He told himself to get over it. It wasn't as if she was sending out friendly vibes.

Just the opposite. She was pricklier than a porcupine, and he sensed she'd rather be on her own.

Since he pretty much sucked at relationships with women, or so he'd been told by two previous girlfriends, Rock told himself to be glad Hailey wasn't displaying any personal interest in him. His only job was to keep her safe.

They hiked for twenty minutes before he insisted on taking another break. They sat at the base of a tree. Once again, he offered Hailey his canteen, and she took a sip before handing it back. He couldn't explain why her prolonged silence was beginning to get on his nerves. He should be grateful, not annoyed.

Hailey sniffed the air, then rose to her feet. He frowned, wondering what had caught her attention.

She eased through the thick brush, her gaze sweeping the ground. Curious, he joined her. "What is it?"

"Black bear scat." She gestured to a brown pile. "Relatively fresh in my estimation."

"Good nose you have there. I agree with your assessment, that was left within the past few hours." Bears were not uncommon in the Smoky Mountains, but he was surprised she'd picked up on it. "Based on the size, it's from a large bear. Let's just hope it's not a momma with her cub."

"Yeah." Hailey's gaze raked the area. "Nothing worse than facing a mad momma."

She sounded as if she might be speaking from experience, which only piqued his curiosity. "Let's rest a bit." He gestured back to the large tree. "I'd like to reach the cabin before dusk."

Her brow furrowed. "It's that far from here?"

"It's not that far, ten minutes by trail, but longer for us since we're cutting through the brush."

She flushed. "Okay, that makes sense. I guess I'll have to trust your skills as a park ranger."

It occurred to him that he hadn't introduced himself. "Rock."

"Huh?" She looked at the boulder, then back at him, confused.

"My name is Rock. Rock Wilson."

There was a brief pause. "Interesting name."

He was used to the comments about why on earth any parent would name their kid *Rock*. "Technically, my name is Rick, short for Richard, but my younger sister couldn't pronounce it, so the nickname Rock stuck."

A ghost of a smile crossed her features. "That's cute." She fell silent again without offering anything personal about herself in return, which was as interesting as it was frustrating.

Who was Hailey Donovan?

And why had someone tried to kill her?

The hike didn't take as long as he'd feared. Within fifteen minutes, he made out the rough-hewn walls of the abandoned cabin.

Being so close to shelter infused him with a spurt of renewed energy. He picked up the pace, glad his sense of direction hadn't failed him. Dusk was just beginning to fall, and that was the time wildlife emerged to hunt.

He wasn't interested in being viewed as some animal's dinner.

"Is there a water source nearby?" It was the first time Hailey had spoken since their last rest stop.

"Yes. But let's check the cabin first while there's still enough light to see."

She nodded and followed as he went over to the sagging door. He had to shove at it with his shoulder to wedge it open enough for them to get through.

The interior was dim, the windows covered with dirt, grime, and moss. It looked much like he remembered, and not nearly as comforting as he'd hoped.

"Any food?" Hailey headed over to the area that had once served as the kitchen.

"Doubtful." He had a couple of power bars that he'd

saved for dinner. He pulled them out of his pocket and set them on the table. "But don't worry, we won't starve."

She gazed at the power bars with interest. "That's a park ranger for you, always prepared."

He grinned. "Just like the Boy Scouts." There wasn't any furniture other than a rickety chair leaning up against the wall. He reached over and grabbed it, bringing it over to the table.

A hiss followed by the distinctive sound of a rattler echoed through the room. He froze, as did Hailey.

A poisonous timber rattlesnake had claimed first dibs on the cabin.

## CHAPTER TWO

Hailey had to give the park ranger credit. Rock reacted instinctively by shoving her behind him and reaching for his gun.

"If you shoot the snake, the gunman will know where we are," she murmured. "I thought the point of coming here was to remain hidden?"

"It is." He glanced at her over his shoulder. Even though the sunlight barely filtered through the dirt-streaked windows, she could see that his expression was grim. "But I'm sure you realize this thing is deadly. Why, did you have another idea?"

"We could try to get it out of here with a couple of sticks." It wasn't a fail-safe method, she would rather have had a large machete to chop its head off, but she hadn't thought to bring one with her.

Looking back, she should have brought food and other supplies on her hike. Although she hadn't intended to be gone very long.

And she certainly hadn't expected to be the target of some idiot's gunfire.

She must be slipping at the ripe old age of twenty-seven. Normally, she'd have been prepared for anything. Having a stable job and a place to live for the past couple of years had made her soft.

The rattler grew louder, as if the snake was irritated with them invading his space and wanted them gone. Normally, she'd be happy to oblige. But there had been a threat of rain in the forecast, and staying in the cabin would offer some protection from the elements.

The last thing she wanted was to cozy up next to Rock.

Rock backed up a step, bumping into her. She steadied herself with a hand on his back. "Listen, I have an idea. We can use the bear scat to chase him out," she whispered. "Snakes hate strong smells."

"Hard to blame them. And we'll be stuck with the smell too," Rock pointed out.

"I'll find a large pile of leaves to bring it in here, and once the snake is gone, I'll get rid of it." Sounded easier said than done, but she wasn't about to let that deter her. "Stay here, I'll be back soon."

"Be careful and keep your head down, Hailey," Rock said dryly. "The goal here is to keep you safe, remember? Don't give the guy with the rifle the chance to take another shot at you."

"I won't." She wasn't the least bit worried about that. The snake was the biggest threat at the moment.

"I'll try to hold off shooting the rattler if at all possible."

"Good plan." Hailey slipped through the narrow opening of the cabin door and retraced their steps to where she'd seen the black bear droppings. As the sun dipped lower on the horizon, it was harder to see, but following her nose worked. Soon she found what they'd stumbled across earlier.

This was the icky part. Wrinkling her nose, she scraped together a pile of leaves and managed to get enough of the bear scat scooped up to hopefully get the stupid rattler out of the cabin.

"Super gross," she muttered as she carried it back to the cabin. At least she hadn't heard the sound of any more gunfire, from the original shooter or Rock.

"Is that you, Hailey?" Rock called as she approached. The guy must have bat ears because she knew how to move silently through the woods.

"Yeah. Coming through with smelly stuff," she warned.

"Oh yippee," he drawled.

She found herself smiling, a rare occurrence, at his sarcasm. She slid in through the narrow opening. Taking a moment to allow her eyesight to adjust to the dim lighting, she found the location of the rattler. He was nestled in the farthest corner of the cabin, catty-corner from the doorway.

Now, all she had to do was get the bear scat nearby and hopefully shoo Mr. Timber Rattler toward the door. Easy peasy, right?

Rock had a large, long stick in his hand that he was wielding in an attempt to draw the snake toward him. Since he was distracting the reptile, she crept around and set the smelly leaf pile as close to the snake as possible.

The snake's hissing and rattling grew impossibly louder, and the reptile carefully uncoiled itself, his tiny head reaching up higher and higher.

It was creepy. She'd always hated snakes.

Waving the stick, Rock walked backward toward the door. Impossibly, the snake followed, slithering across the cabin floor. Maybe the strong scent emanating from the bear droppings helped him move on, but she knew the ranger's stick-wielding prowess also played an important role in getting the thing to move.

Soon, it was just Hailey and the snake inside the cabin. Rock was outside, still drawing the snake's attention with the stick in an attempt to coax it through the narrow opening. Breathing through her mouth, she used her hiking shoe to push the leaf pile closer to the tail end of the snake.

The timber rattler's head abruptly spun toward her with frightening speed, the tiny forked tongue darting out, making her jump back and plaster herself against the wall. Her heart pounded, but the reptile reared away from the bear scent. It slithered through the opening of the door and disappeared from sight.

Hailey sagged against the wall, breathing a deep sigh of relief.

*Gee, that was fun,* she thought as she pushed away from the cabin wall to bend down and lift the pile of stinky leaves off the floor.

Rock came in, moving aside so she could edge past him to get rid of the bear scat. The unmistakable scent, however, still lingered in the air.

She hoped it would dissipate soon. Thankfully, the place was hardly airtight, plenty of cracks and crevices for fresh air to seep in. Rock went through the rest of the cabin, making sure there were no additional unwelcome surprises, before turning toward her. "Guess we should find that water source."

"Yeah, washing my hands would be nice." And so would taking several breaths of fresh air.

"I have some sanitizer too," he offered.

"Good." She was glad to hear it. "I'll use that after I wash up in the creek."

"Follow me." Now that the imminent danger of the deadly snake was gone, Rock confidently led the way out of the cabin. They went several yards before she heard the soft trickle of water.

One good thing about being stuck in the Smoky Mountains was that the water supply was plentiful and of decent quality. The high humidity was responsible for the smoky mist that generally hung around the mountains in the mornings and evenings, and that mist helped keep the water fresh and potable.

She washed her hands as much as possible, before using a small squirt of Rock's sanitizer, then cupped her hands to drink from the stream. He drank, too, and filled his canteen. She was bummed she'd lost her water bottle over the side of the ridge, but there was nothing she could do about that now.

The sun slipped lower behind the dense trees. They'd be in complete darkness very soon, and she found herself wondering why she'd agreed to stay in the cabin with Rock for the night. It wasn't like her.

For one thing, she generally didn't trust men. And for another, she had better wilderness skills than anyone she knew. Well, except maybe for a park ranger.

But all of that aside, her biggest concern was fending off Rock's questions about her personal life. Or his prying into her past. He might be a ranger, but he was also considered a member of law enforcement.

Her previous encounter with a cop hadn't gone well. Hence her juvenile record.

Yet she could appreciate that he'd come to her rescue. It had been a long time since anyone had done that for her. Thirteen years, in fact, since the night of the fire when her foster brother Sawyer and foster sister Jayme had helped her get the rest of the kids out of the cellar of the burning cabin.

She was the one who'd smelled the smoke first and had quickly woken the others. Thankfully, they'd been able to escape mere seconds before the entire place had been engulfed in flames. As much as they'd wanted to stay together, the Preacher and his wife had died in the fire and the cops had begun searching for them. Every last one of them had vowed to never go into foster care again. As a result, they'd split up into groups, Jayme, the oldest, taking Caitlin, the youngest. Hailey and Darby had gone one way. The three boys—Sawyer, Cooper, and Trent—had gone yet another.

She'd been closest to Sawyer at the time, as they were the same age, but she hadn't seen him in years. Really, she hadn't seen any of the fosters. After a horrible argument with Darby, her foster sister had taken off. Then Hailey had been arrested for stealing. After getting out of juvie, Hailey had tried to find Darby, but after she'd failed to find a trace of her sister anywhere, sheer survival had eventually caused her to worry about her own life.

Yet, Darby's disappearance still haunted her. Especially because Darby's last words were how much she hated Hailey.

Hailey had no positive memories of those years running and hiding from the system. As far as she was concerned, it was all best left buried deep in the past.

"Hailey? Are you okay?"

"Huh? Oh, yeah." She gathered her scattered thoughts. "Let's go."

They made their way back to the dilapidated cabin.

The only good thing about the structure was that it helped shield them from the elements.

Once Hailey would have preferred to sleep beneath the trees, with nothing between her and the dark sky. All those years of being stuck in the cellar had given her a bad case of claustrophobia.

"Take a power bar." Rock held one out to her. "It's all we have for dinner."

"Thanks." She accepted the nourishment, as she would have done the same if she'd have brought anything along. "What's the plan come morning?"

He shrugged, although she couldn't really see him very well in the dark interior of the cabin. "Hike down to the road, I guess. I highly doubt the shooter will have stayed out there all night, waiting for you."

Maybe, maybe not. Hailey thought that it depended on who had tried to shoot her and why. Did the shooter know her personally? If so, he or she likely knew where her trailer was located. And, therefore, staying overnight in the mountains wouldn't matter much.

He could always try again.

It was a puzzle, for sure. Especially since she didn't understand who could be holding a grudge against her all this time. Darby had been extremely angry, but to let that fester this long seemed crazy. Yet there wasn't another person on the planet she'd been close to, other than Darby.

After finishing her power bar, she made her way over to the far side of the cabin, opposite from where Rock was seated. Without saying anything, she curled up on the hard floor, her back against the wall, and cushioned her head beneath her elbow.

"Hailey?" Rock's soft voice made her want to sigh.

"What?" Her tone wasn't exactly inviting.

"You're absolutely sure you don't know anyone who'd want to hurt you?"

"If I did, I'd say something so you could arrest the jerk," she said wearily, instinctively shying away from mentioning Darby. "Do you think I like being used for target practice? I don't. But the only person I so much as yelled at in the recent past was Owen, the seven-year-old who pinched Rory the donkey."

"Okay, just—" Rock hesitated, then said, "After we get off the mountain, keep your eyes open and alert for any hint of danger."

Really? Did he think she hadn't figured that out for herself? She managed to hold back her sarcasm. Rock was only trying to help. Her lousy attitude wasn't his fault.

"I will. Good night." Hailey closed her eyes and willed herself to sleep.

But it wasn't easy. She'd gotten soft over the years and found it difficult to relax on the hard and uneven floor. Which was strange since she'd slept on the unforgiving floor of the cellar in the Preacher's cabin for five long years.

She squeezed her eyes shut and forced her mind to happier subjects. Her last thought before she dozed off was that she'd have to find a way to let Nora Rhodes know she'd be late to work the following morning.

Hailey didn't want to lose her job of working with animals. At this point, they were her only salvation.

---

ROCK WAS SHOCKED when Hailey simply stretched out on the floor and went to sleep. No woman he'd ever known would do something like that, especially without complaining.

There was something mysterious about Hailey Donovan, and he couldn't seem to rein in his blatant curiosity about her.

Not that she'd said much about herself. Quite the opposite. Every question felt like pulling teeth to elicit a response.

In his experience, that meant she had something to hide. Yet he also didn't see Hailey as the type not to stick up for herself. To let an attempted murderer go free.

No, he didn't think she'd allow something like that, yet she might try to take care of things by herself. The word *loner* may as well have been tattooed on her forehead for the entire world to see.

Which only deepened his curiosity about her. Who was Hailey Donovan, and why would someone try to shoot her? He thought back, remembering there had been three separate gunshots.

Three attempts to take her down wasn't an accident. And it was only because of the grace of God and His master plan that she was still alive.

A plan Rock was now a part of, as much as she was.

He shifted on the floor, wincing a bit. He was getting too old for this kind of roughing it.

To preserve the battery life of his phone, he'd shut it down after verifying one last time there was no service. Rock knew his fellow park rangers would be trying to reach him via the radio and mentally kicked himself for losing it.

Then again, he wasn't used to being shot at.

He'd arrested several poachers in his seven years as a ranger, along with a handful of goofball kids who didn't seem to understand the concept that shooting small game had to be done in season and required a license.

But standing alongside a woman while someone tried to kill her was a first for him.

And hopefully the last.

A light rain pelted the roof of the cabin, making Rock glad they'd gotten the rattler out. Sleeping in the rain with just a leafy barrier between them and the clouds wouldn't be fun.

Not that he was having a barrel of laughs regardless.

He shifted again, rolling onto his other side, wondering how in the world Hailey was managing to sleep on the other side of the cabin. The summer nighttime temperature was mild, so it wasn't a matter of needing to share body heat. It was an issue of comfort.

He must have dozed at one point because a soft mewling sound brought him awake. For several long moments he listened intently, hoping and praying the sound hadn't come from a bobcat lurking outside the cabin.

When he heard it again, Rock realized the sound was coming from Hailey. He sat up, rubbed his hands over his face, and silently rose to his feet.

Moving as quietly as possible, he approached Hailey's curled form. As he grew closer, he understood she was saying, "No, no, please, no," in a whimpering tone.

His heart squeezed in his chest as he realized she was having a nightmare. And the idea that she may have suffered some sort of abuse, physical or sexual, wouldn't leave him alone.

"No!" Hailey's abrupt scream sent him stumbling back a step. In the dim light, he could see she'd bolted upright off the floor, her hands up in front of her face.

"Hailey, it's me, Rock. You're okay, we're spending the night in the cabin, remember?"

For long seconds she didn't say a word, although he

could hear her heavy breathing and gasping, as if she'd been running for her life.

Which, for all he knew, maybe she was. Literally and figuratively.

And if that was the case, there was the distinct possibility she knew more about the gunfire than she'd let on.

"Sorry if I woke you," she finally murmured. She sat with her back up against the cabin wall, her knees drawn up to her chest, her arms wrapped around them as if it took all her strength to hold herself together.

"You didn't," he lied. "I'm out of practice sleeping on the floor."

"Me too," she agreed.

It was the first time she'd mentioned anything remotely personal. And he wasn't surprised to learn she used to sleep on the ground. Frankly, she was better at it than he was.

He wished he knew more about her.

"At least we're out of the rain," she added.

"Right?" He let out a low chuckle. "Good thing we got rid of Mr. Timber Rattler."

"Yeah." She fell silent, as if running out of things to say.

"How about a sip of water?" He turned and grabbed the canteen he'd left on the small table, then offered it to her.

Hailey hesitated a moment, then accepted the canteen and took a small sip. "Thanks."

"Care to tell me about it?" He strove to keep his tone casual.

"No." Her blunt response wasn't unexpected. After all, why would Hailey confide in him now?

"Okay." He took a sip from the canteen as well, then recapped it and set it on the table. Instead of heading back to the opposite side of the room, though, he dropped down about two feet from where she was sitting.

"I'm fine," she said curtly.

"I know." He admired her steely determination but felt that anyone who'd had the kind of nightmare that caused her to scream out in terror, waking her from a sound sleep, needed someone close by.

Whether she liked it or not.

## CHAPTER THREE

—————

Mortified at waking Rock with her nightmare, Hailey wrapped her arms around her knees, buried her face in her arms, and pulled herself together with an effort.

It had been years since she'd suffered nightmares, or more aptly, flashbacks of her time with the Preacher. It had been thirteen years since she'd been free of him, but sometimes it felt like yesterday.

She was twenty-seven now, not fourteen. A grown woman, not a scared kid. She still didn't understand how the Preacher had gotten away with treating her and the other foster kids the way he had. Yet she remembered all too clearly how sweet and nice the Preacher and Ruth acted when the social worker arrived for their so-called surprise visits. And frankly, it wasn't often that the state bothered to send anyone at all.

No one suspected the man who'd carried his Bible everywhere and acted kind and generous in public would turn into a horrific monster, the very devil he constantly preached about, in private.

The state-employed caseworkers hadn't known how the

Preacher had hit them with a switch even as he shouted passages from the Bible, screaming that they were all sinners and going to hell. As if that wasn't bad enough, he'd forced them to kneel and recite passages back to him until their kneecaps were raw and bleeding, their backs and shoulders aching and sore from being bent over and absorbing blow after blow.

He'd forced them to sleep in the dank, dark cellar, which had almost become their tomb when the fire broke out. She still wasn't sure how they'd escaped certain death that day.

Beads of sweat popped out on her forehead, and she gave herself a mental shake. No. Not here, not now. She'd worked hard to bury those awful memories so she could focus on the life she was living. She had a future now.

She was free.

Maybe it was lying on the cold, hard floor that had brought the horrible memories rushing back. Still, it was embarrassing, and she was glad Rock hadn't pushed the issue.

Although she knew he'd wanted to.

Rock sat beside her, almost within arm's reach. Disturbingly close, but she didn't have the energy to get up and move away.

If he moved any closer, she would, but he didn't. After what seemed like hours, but was probably only twenty to thirty minutes, she shifted her position so she was once again lying on her side along the floor, her back pressed against the wall, and cradling her head in the crook of her elbow.

Closing her eyes, she tried to clear her mind and sleep. It wasn't easy to figure out what time it was, but she figured they had a couple of hours yet before the sun rose. They wouldn't hit the trail until they could see well enough to navigate through the woods. The last thing she needed was to trip and break a leg. Or her neck.

She tried to clear her mind, but it was no use. The dream hovered in the back of her subconscious, despite her efforts to push it away. She thought about Rory the kicking donkey, Lucy the spitting llama, and the other animals at Nora's hobby farm. Working there for the past five years had been her salvation. It was depressing to realize she wouldn't be able to feed them bright and early in the morning. She enjoyed getting there early, to have those hours with the animals all to herself.

Even thinking about the animals she liked better than most people didn't relax her enough to fall asleep. Ignoring the hunger pangs in her belly was easy enough, she'd had a lot of practice skipping meals. What was very different and not at all easy to ignore was having Rock within arm's reach. She smiled grimly in the darkness when she heard his soft even breathing.

Guess it was a good thing one of them was resting.

Her thoughts went back to the other foster kids she'd lived with during those years with the Preacher. Specifically Sawyer, who'd been her age when they'd managed to escape, and Darby, two years her junior, who'd disappeared likely with her boyfriend, Aaron, when Hailey had gotten arrested.

Cooper, Trent, Jayme, and little Caitlin too.

What were they doing now? Were they safe and healthy?

Or had they gotten themselves into trouble, the way she had? If the latter, she hoped they'd found a way to turn their lives around.

The way she'd attempted to do. Not as successfully as she'd have liked, but better than she could have imagined.

A sense of hopelessness washed over her. Hailey knew getting maudlin wouldn't help her sleep, but her secret wish was that one day she'd meet up with at least one of her foster siblings.

And that they'd be okay, alive and reasonably well, the way she'd finally gotten to be.

Thanks in large part to Nora and finding solace with the animals.

When the barest hint of light could be seen through the dirt-streaked windows, Hailey eased herself upright and silently moved across the cabin toward the door, being careful not to wake Rock.

Outside, the heavy mist hung in the air, seeming to drip from the leaves of the trees. Hailey took a deep breath, cleansing her mind and her senses.

After a quick nature call, she returned to the cabin. It had been tempting to simply leave, knowing Rock could find his way back on his own.

She didn't quite know why she hadn't, other than sensing he'd have just tried to follow her anyway. Better she cooperated with him for a little while longer.

Oddly enough, Rock was one of the few men she'd been able to spend time with. Granted, he hadn't asked much of her and had kept his distance, but still, she couldn't deny that he didn't annoy her as much as others she'd spent time with.

Including her ex-boyfriend, Jacob.

"There you are." Rock's voice coming from behind her nearly made her jump out of her skin. She whirled and glared at him.

"Why'd you sneak up on me like that?" Her previous kind feelings toward him vanished in a nanosecond.

"I wasn't trying to be sneaky," he protested mildly. "To be honest, I thought you were leaving without me."

Since the thought had been on her mind, she couldn't find fault with his logic. "I'm still here, aren't I?" she asked testily.

"Yeah." Rock tipped his head back and looked at the mist hanging overhead. "Visibility will be lousy on the trail," he observed.

"I know."

"I saved two power bars for breakfast." He eyed her speculatively. "We'll eat first, then head out. But we need to move slow, to avoid a catastrophic injury."

"I know," she repeated. "Despite how things look, I'm not a novice hiker."

"Never said you were," Rock drawled. "In fact, I'd say you're a pro, better than anyone I've met in the recent months."

His comment shouldn't have pleased her, but it did. To ward off the sappy feeling, she slipped into the cabin and crossed over to the table where he'd left the last two power bars.

She picked them up and turned to hand him one. "Thanks for this," she said as she unwrapped it.

"You're welcome."

A single power bar had never tasted so good, and even that small amount of food gave her the burst of energy she'd need to hike out of there.

Although returning to her trailer wouldn't be the end of things. Not if the shooter had targeted her on purpose. The idea made her frown. Jacob had left on his own, she couldn't imagine he was harboring some sort of resentment toward her.

Maybe one of the foster kids? Darby? Her foster sister had been incredibly angry when she had stormed out of their flea-infested motel. The thought of Darby seeking revenge after all this time made her stomach clench. It didn't make sense, but then nothing else did either. And if that was the case, she wouldn't rat her sister out.

No matter what.

"You have phone service up here?" she asked when she'd finished the power bar and had taken a sip of water. "I need to call my boss to let her know I'll be late for work."

"No, but I'll keep trying," Rock assured her. "The Beaver Trail isn't far. When we find that, we should have better luck with hitting a cell tower."

"Okay, let's do it." She was anxious to be on the move. All this togetherness was too—well, *intimate*, for lack of a better word.

Rock led the way toward the Beaver Trail. She didn't mind letting him go first, being outside in the fresh air was all she needed.

"At least the shooter can't see us," she joked as they went through a particularly dense area of fog.

"That's one way to look on the bright side," Rock shot back. "Watch your step, I don't want to be forced to carry you out of here."

"Same goes, I wouldn't want to carry you out of here either," she retorted.

"As if you could," he said with a chuckle. "I'm twice your size."

"I'm stronger than I look." Working on a hobby farm had honed her muscles over the past five years. And she'd hiked the mountains often, keeping up her stamina.

"Tougher too," he agreed. Then he abruptly stopped and held up a hand.

She froze, wondering if he'd stumbled across another snake or some other wild animal. He was armed, but she hoped he didn't have to shoot anything with two or four legs.

As far as she was concerned, snakes didn't count. They didn't have legs.

After a few long, agonizing moments, Rock lowered his hand. "Bobcat," he whispered. "It's moved on now."

"I wouldn't have minded seeing it," she said in a low voice. "Not that I want to meet one up close and personal, mind you."

"I understand, they are amazing creatures. But I didn't want to risk cubs being nearby." Rock continued walking. It was almost twenty minutes when they reached the Beaver Trail. He paused, pulled out his cell phone, and powered it up.

She edged close, peering over his shoulder to see if he had a signal. When he turned to face her, she was close enough to see tiny flecks of gold in his hazel eyes.

"I think it'll work, if you want to call your boss," he said, offering her the phone.

"Thanks." She blamed her breathlessness on relief of having a way to talk to Nora rather than on Rock's closeness. Nora answered on the first ring.

"Hey, it's Hailey. I'm sorry, but I'll be late for work this morning."

"What's wrong?" Nora demanded. "Are you sick?"

"I'm fine, just tied up," she hastened to assure her. "I'll fill you in later, okay? I'll try to get there before the first bus arrives at nine."

"Okay, if you're sure you're all right." Nora clearly was

taken aback by the early call. Likely because Hailey had never been late for work before.

"I promise I'm fine. Later." She disconnected and handed Rock's phone back. "Thanks for letting me call. She'd have worried if she hadn't heard from me."

"It's not a problem." Rock eyed her thoughtfully as he tucked the phone into his pocket. "Ready to keep going?"

"Of course."

Rock once again led the way, leaving Hailey to follow. As they continued along the trail, which was much easier to navigate compared to hiking through the dense brush, it occurred to her she might actually miss Rock when she was back home.

Which was completely ridiculous, considering she knew next to nothing about the man.

Other than he was probably the nicest guy she'd ever spent the night with.

---

ROCK COULD TELL from hearing Hailey's part of the conversation that it was unusual for her to be late or miss work.

He admired a strong work ethic but thought most people would call off for a shift if they'd been forced to spend the night on the floor of an abandoned mountain cabin. Especially after being used for target practice.

It was easy to admire Hailey, even while being irritated that she hadn't been completely honest with him. She must know something about why she'd been targeted. Bad guys didn't randomly pick women to shoot at.

Yet trying to get Hailey to open up was like trying to pry open a vise with nothing but your fingernails. The woman could have a career in the Pentagon; he sincerely doubted she'd confide any secrets about her past.

Although the little bit he'd overheard of her nightmare bothered him. She'd sounded like a wounded animal, and he was a man who took pride in allowing wild animals to survive and thrive.

"What bus arrives at nine?" he asked, thinking the hobby farm was a neutral topic.

"Another group of kids from a local day care," she said with a sigh. "The younger ones are generally pretty good with the animals, but every so often we get saddled with an Owen."

He nodded, glancing at her over his shoulder. "The boy who pinches donkeys."

"Yeah." A flash of humor crossed her features. "He wasn't too happy when Lucy spit at him."

"And Lucy is," he paused, then guessed, "a llama?"

"You know your animals," she said with approval. "Yes, Lucy is our youngest llama. Some of the older ones can be used to give rides to kids under the age of six, but not Lucy. She despises all humans."

"Which probably makes you like her all the more," he said.

Her grin widened, and she didn't bother to deny it. "We have goats too. Those are an overall favorite. The kids love to feed them."

He was vaguely aware of Nora Rhodes's hobby farm, but he hadn't spent any time there. "How did you end up working for Nora?"

She shrugged and glanced away. "I was hiking through the area and needed a job. I also liked animals. Nora's college student quit without notice. I saw her help wanted sign, and she hired me on."

He waited several minutes for her to expound on that, but she didn't. Why he suspected there was more to that story, he wasn't sure.

Not his business. Unless, of course, the shooting was somehow related to Hailey's work on the farm. Which didn't seem likely. The sobering reality was that he'd likely never know the outcome of Hailey's problems.

His jurisdiction as a park ranger only went so far. The crime had taken place on federal national parkland, but they weren't staffed for this type of investigation. They'd usually partner with the locals on something like this.

"Hailey, you'll need to get in touch with the local law enforcement to report yesterday's shooting."

"Yeah, probably." Her response didn't inspire confidence in her intent to follow through.

He frowned at her. "It's important, especially if there's another attempt to hurt you."

She shrugged and nodded. "Okay, but I can guarantee they won't do anything about it."

"Why not?" Her response shocked him.

Hailey didn't answer for a long moment. "Just speaking from past experience."

Most law enforcement officers he knew would take someone shooting at a woman very seriously. Although he knew there was a bad apple or two in the bunch.

"I'll call them," she repeated. "You're right, it's better to have the attempt on record."

"I'll make note of it as well," he said in an effort to reassure her. "And like I said, the rangers will be on the lookout for anything suspicious."

"Thanks."

Hiking the Beaver Trail down to the main road didn't

take as long as he feared. The closer they got to the road, the more bars on his phone.

He'd need to call a colleague to come pick him up since his vehicle was a good ten miles from here. Normally he didn't mind hiking ten miles, he did a lot of trail walking as he scouted for poachers.

But he was tired and hungry. And he needed to replace his lost radio. He grimaced, hoping the cost wouldn't be deducted from his paycheck.

As they approached the road, tension seemed to radiate off Hailey. "Is there a problem?" he finally asked.

"No."

"Yeah, right." If she thought she was fooling him, she was sorely mistaken. "Listen, I'll call a ranger friend of mine to come pick us up. We can give you a lift to wherever you left your vehicle."

"I didn't realize the Beaver Trail came out here." She gestured to the space where the path met the road. "I don't live far, I can walk."

"How far?" He wasn't about to let her walk ten miles, especially since they still didn't know for sure where the shooter had been standing when he'd taken the shots.

"Less than a mile."

"Really? Would you mind giving me a ride to my vehicle then? I'm parked ten miles from here."

There was a long pause as she considered his request. He glanced at her, noting the indecision reflected in her clear blue eyes.

"If you wouldn't mind, it would save me some time," he pressed.

"Sure. Although my truck is nothing fancy."

"I don't mind, thanks." He grinned at getting the prickly porcupine to agree to giving him a lift.

From the little he knew about Hailey, he sensed she didn't mingle much with people. Although if she changed her mind, he'd be in trouble. A quick glance at his phone showed he only had about 15 percent of juice left on its battery.

Once they reached the road, she turned to the right. He followed, wondering where her trailer was located. She'd mentioned living in the Whispering Oaks Trailer Park, but he wasn't familiar with it.

Hailey didn't say much of anything as they walked along the road. When he saw the dilapidated sign for the Whispering Oaks Trailer Park, he tried not to grimace.

No doubt Hailey was sensitive about where she lived. And who was he to pass judgment? The small cabin he called home wasn't anything fancy.

"I can pay you for gas," he offered as they crossed the road and approached the trailer park.

"Not necessary. You provided dinner and breakfast," she added with a cheeky grin.

She had a great sense of humor when she allowed herself to relax. "I hardly think a couple of power bars counts as two meals."

"They were better than nothing," she countered. When she approached a brown and white trailer, her steps slowed.

He caught the grim expression on her features. "What is it?"

"The front door is ajar." She abruptly sprinted toward the trailer, leaving him eating her dust as he followed.

She threw open the door and barreled inside before he could shout at her to wait.

Then she stopped so quickly he was surprised she didn't fall on her face. When he came up behind her and looked over her shoulder, he understood.

The interior of the trailer was trashed—sofa cushions slashed, dishes broken, and clothing tossed around, much of it destroyed.

He put his arm around her shoulders. "Are you absolutely sure you don't know who tried to shoot at you?"

She dumbly shook her head.

"Whoever it is, he or she knows exactly who you are." He surveyed the mess grimly. "And they're clearly mad at you about something."

Hailey didn't say a word in response. She shook off his arm, spun on her heel, and edged past him to stride toward her truck.

And her silence in the face of the violence against her bothered him most of all.

## CHAPTER FOUR

*Someone hates me enough to kill me.*

The destruction of her trailer bespoke of sheer rage and unsuppressed fury. Seeing it shook her to the core. She didn't have many possessions, certainly nothing from those horrible years with the Preacher, but she doubted the few small things she'd gathered over the years had survived the angry and very personal assault.

*Darby.*

She didn't want to believe it. It didn't make any sense, but this was clearly personal. She strode toward her truck, her mind whirling. Hearing Rock coming up behind her, she paused at the door of her rusty Chevy.

"Hailey, wait. Where are you going?" Rock's deep husky voice penetrated her thoughts.

She frowned. "You asked for a lift to your vehicle, remember?"

He stared at her as if she'd sprouted a third eye. "We're not going anywhere until you call the police."

She inwardly grimaced. Why did he have to be such a cop? "Maybe I'm just messy."

"Stop it." His harsh tone raked over her, making her feel foolish. "Someone took three shots at you, and now your home has been trashed. Call the local police or I will."

It galled her to admit he was right. While she normally avoided any interaction with the cops, she knew he wasn't going to let this go. With a grimace, she gestured toward his phone. "I'll need to borrow yours. Mine was inside the trailer." And likely smashed to smithereens.

Thankfully, it was a disposable phone and not worth much anyway.

Rock didn't hesitate to hand her his phone. "There's not a lot of battery life left, so make it quick."

She stared at the screen for a moment. "I don't know the nonemergency number."

"Call 911, for all we know, the person who did this is still hanging around."

With reluctance, she dialed the emergency number, a first for her. When the dispatcher answered, she tried to be concise. "My name is Hailey Donovan. I live in trailer number thirteen in the Whispering Oaks Trailer Park outside of Gatlinburg. My trailer has been broken into and wrecked. Also, someone took several shots at me last evening. I'm here at the trailer with Park Ranger Rock Wilson."

The dispatcher repeated most of the key information, maybe as she was typing it into a computer. Hailey tried not to show her impatience at the length of the call. If they didn't hurry up, she'd never make it to Nora's in time to meet the nine o'clock bus.

Finally, the dispatcher said, "I'm sending an officer to your location."

"Thanks." She disconnected from the line and scowled. "This is going to take way too much time."

Rock stared at her incredulously. "Hailey, this is serious stuff. Can you imagine what might have happened if you'd been here last night?"

She sighed and nodded. "Yeah, I know. But standing around all morning talking to the police isn't going to help find whoever did this."

"What would help is for you to stop lying," Rock retorted.

She sucked in a harsh breath, then glowered at him. "I haven't lied to you."

"Omitting potentially relevant facts in an ongoing investigation is considered a falsehood," Rock retorted. "Stop playing games, Hailey, and tell me who you think is behind this."

She pressed her lips together, unable to turn on her foster sibling. Darby was the only one she'd fought with, albeit ten years ago. Was it possible being with Aaron had turned her foster sister into a criminal? If Darby had somehow returned to the area, found Hailey, and set out to kill her, they'd never find her. One thing all the fosters had learned extremely well, especially after the fire, was how to disappear into the wooded mist and fly under the radar. "Jacob Rokeby is an old boyfriend. You can try him, although as I said, he left me for another woman, so I'm not sure he gives a hoot about what I'm doing."

Rock simply stared at her, his penetrating hazel gaze impossible to ignore. She tilted her chin and defiantly met his gaze.

It would be impossible for anyone to understand what the seven foster kids had gone through. How surviving the horror had brought them together in a way that was similar to groups of men who fought together in battle. They'd all been so close once.

But not anymore.

If Darby was seeking some sort of revenge all these years later, then so be it. She couldn't, wouldn't turn on her sister. Besides, Hailey's best chance to stay alive would be to find Darby herself. Maybe if she faced her sister one-on-one, they could hash out whatever anger Darby might be harboring toward her.

And if that didn't work? Then she'd give up her life for Darby's. Because she couldn't sit by and watch her sister go to jail for an emotional breakdown that wasn't her fault.

If the Preacher was still alive, she'd readily bring charges against him. Unfortunately, you couldn't arrest and jail a ghost.

Rock didn't let up, clearly waiting for her to break down and start talking.

He'd be waiting a very, very long time. The one virtue the Preacher had instilled in them was patience. She could sit or stand in one place for hours without moving.

The sound of a police siren broke the strained tension between them. Hailey turned to watch the squad approach. She walked back toward her trailer as the cop pulled up. Rock followed but stayed back, letting her take the lead.

For now. She had no doubt that if she didn't tell the authorities every last detail, he wouldn't hesitate to step in and fill in the gaps.

"Ms. Donovan?" A burly officer slid out from behind the wheel. He was at least ten years older than she was and overweight, his belly hanging over his belt buckle. She didn't make the mistake of believing his girth made him soft.

Instead, she had to swallow hard against the bile that rose in her throat. He reminded her too much of the cop who'd arrested her for stealing ten years ago.

"Yes." She waited for him to introduce himself.

"Officer Morrison, with the Gatlinburg PD." Officer Morrison glanced over her shoulder at Rock. "And you must be Ranger Wilson."

"Yes." She almost smiled at Rock's clipped response. He didn't appear too impressed with Officer Morrison, and for some reason, she found herself pleased with Rock's assessment.

"You called about a break-in and gunfire?" Morrison asked.

"That's my trailer, number thirteen." She gestured toward it. "The door was hanging ajar when we approached. You can go in and see for yourself, we didn't touch anything other than the front door."

"We?" She wanted to smack Morrison's leering face.

"Ms. Donovan was hiking last evening when someone took several shots at her," Rock said sharply. "One of the shots almost hit me. We took refuge in an abandoned cabin for the night and, upon our returning home this morning, found Ms. Donovan's home destroyed."

Morrison's leering grin disappeared in the face of Rock's strident tone. "Any idea where the gunfire came from?"

"A rifle, maybe a thirty-aught-six, from the northeast," Rock replied. "Shooter clearly had a scope but failed to hit his or her target, so not sure how much experience they had."

"I see." Morrison nodded, then walked toward the trailer. "Unlucky thirteen," he muttered as he drew on a pair of gloves.

"Thirteen is my favorite number," she shot back. Maybe it was the lack of sleep, or the way her stomach was growling, but she was finding it hard to hold back her annoyance.

"Not anymore now, is it?" Officer Morrison opened the door and went inside.

"Jerk," she muttered.

"Yeah," Rock agreed. She glanced at him in surprise. "It annoys me that the good ole boy club still runs strong in this part of the state."

Again, she was impressed by his attitude. She considered herself a good judge of character, and Rock struck her as a decent guy. At some level, she knew that was the reason she'd stayed in the cabin with him.

Although now she wished she hadn't. If Rock wouldn't have been there, she'd have gone to work and dealt with the mess of her trailer later.

She wanted to leave, to get far away from here. And why not? It wouldn't be the first time she'd reinvent herself to start someplace new. For years, she'd survived by being constantly on the move. It had served her well in the past.

Go where? Do what? For the first time in eons, she liked her job on the hobby farm. Nora was wonderful, and she especially enjoyed working with the animals, despite the occasional pinching Owen.

She didn't want to leave.

Yet if Darby had turned criminal and was out to get her, then maybe she should disappear. Go farther south, toward Chattanooga or through the mountains into North Carolina. She'd miss the mountains but could look for something close to the ocean.

Glancing over to her trailer, she noticed Rock was in a deep discussion with Officer Morrison. Putting her hand in her pocket, she drew out her truck keys and headed toward the vehicle.

She wouldn't leave the area just yet, but she wasn't going to stand around here doing nothing either. She doubted Officer Morrison was going to do much, other than make a note of the damage. He didn't give the impression of being the type of cop that went above and beyond the call of duty.

The way Rock had.

Whatever. It didn't matter, the mess would be here when she returned. In the meantime, she had work to do. Within seconds, she was in her truck and out on the road heading toward Gatlinburg before Rock or Morrison could stop her.

ROCK GROUND his teeth together in frustration as he watched Hailey's Chevy disappear down the road and out of sight. Morrison spoke into his radio, and when Rock realized he was putting out a BOLO on Hailey, he grabbed the radio from him.

"What are you doing?" Rock demanded harshly. "She's the victim here, not the perp."

"We don't know that she didn't do this herself," Officer Morrison sputtered. "These are rental trailers, so the owner needs to be aware of the damage to his rental property."

"Hailey Donovan was with me when she was shot," Rock said, pinning him with a narrow glare. "Don't you dare insinuate I'm lying."

Morrison got all blustery. "Well, she can't just leave. I need her statement."

Rock understood and frankly shared the officer's anger. If he'd known Hailey would take off like that, he'd have done his best to make her stay.

But the simple truth was that she had every right to leave if she wanted. She wasn't under arrest. That she'd taken off burned his britches, but what could he say? If anything, he should have anticipated such a stunt from her.

"No BOLO," Rock repeated sternly. "I know where she works, and I'm fairly certain that's where she's gone." And left him without a ride to his vehicle.

"Fine, no BOLO," Morrison grudgingly agreed.

"I need a favor, Morrison. My ranger SUV is about ten miles from here. Would you give me a lift?"

Morrison could hardly refuse to help out a fellow peace officer and reluctantly nodded. "What about the crime scene?"

Good question. "It might be helpful to have someone come in and check for fingerprints," he suggested.

"For something as minor as vandalism?" Morrison sneered. "That's a waste of manpower. Besides, I'm not convinced Ms. Donovan didn't do this herself. You know she has a juvie record."

He hadn't known, but on some level he wasn't surprised. But a juvie record didn't mean anything, and the guy's attitude made him want to plant his fist in the man's large gut. Rock held on to his temper with an effort.

"The gunfire that nearly hit her would go down as attempted murder. Seems reasonable to assume the shooter did the damage to her trailer," he pointed out logically. "If she ends up getting hurt or worse, it's going to look bad for you that you didn't have the crime scene taken care of in a proper fashion."

Morrison stared at him, then finally nodded. "Fine. I'll have a crime scene tech come out. But I want that Donovan woman's statement, ASAP. Understand?"

When had he become Hailey Donovan's keeper? Rock inwardly groaned but nodded. After all, he needed a ride to his vehicle. And it was clear Hailey hadn't liked the cop, not that he blamed her. The bottom line here was that it would be better for him to take her in for a statement rather than having Morrison pick her up.

He didn't trust Morrison to handle her like a true victim. And there was something vulnerable about Hailey that bothered him. No way did he think she'd done the damage to her trailer; that was a ridiculous accusation.

Yet the juvie record did explain a few things, primarily her extreme reluctance to call the police in the first place. Then there was the way she'd remained hidden along the trail when he'd approached, along with the moment of hesitation before coming out of the brush to speak with him.

Her nightmare, though, continued to eat at him the most. Was it possible she suffered them as a result of trauma she'd encountered during her stint in juvie? And what on earth had she done to end up there in the first place?

Juvie records were sealed and couldn't be legally accessed without the approval of a judge. Yet he worried that Morrison was just the kind of cop to find a way around pesky rules.

"Ready go to?" Morrison asked, breaking into his troubled thoughts.

"Yeah, thanks." He slid into the passenger seat of Morrison's squad. The trip down to his ranger SUV didn't take long.

"Don't forget, I want that woman's statement," Morrison said as Rock climbed out of the squad.

"I know. Where are your headquarters located? I'll bring Ms. Donovan in as soon as possible."

Morrison gave him the address in Gatlinburg, and Rock committed it to memory. He watched the cop drive away, hoping he'd make good on his promise to have Hailey's trailer treated as a true crime scene.

He slid into the driver's seat, annoyed with the entire

situation. He preferred spending his days in the park, but today would be an exception.

One he didn't appreciate being forced into.

He plugged his phone into his car charger and called in to his team, letting them know that he was fine but unreachable via radio.

"Are you coming in to get a replacement radio?" his boss demanded.

"Soon, I have a few things I need to do first." Rock made a Y-turn on the road to head toward Gatlinburg. "I have to follow up on a few things related to the gunfire aimed at the hiker last evening."

"Hrmph," his boss muttered. "Make it quick. Rumor has it there's another group of poachers on the north side of the park. I need at least three of you covering that area."

There was always a rumor about poachers, but Rock didn't argue. After all, his job as a ranger was to keep the mountains safe from poachers and others who behaved in a way that endangered the wildlife living in the park.

"I will." It was tempting to request time off, simply to help Hailey. He had more than four weeks saved up, but the height of tourist season wasn't the time to request vacation time. Even if he did, his boss likely wouldn't grant it.

Rock used the map app on his phone to pull up the location of the Rhodes Hobby Farm. It was closer than he'd expected, and he arrived about forty minutes after Hailey had left the trailer park.

Seeing her battered Chevy truck confirmed his suspicions. And offered him a bit of relief. She hadn't left town, which was a good thing. Yet while he admired her work ethic, he was still annoyed at the way she'd simply taken off without saying anything.

Leaving him to deal with Morrison.

He parked on the opposite side of the lot since there were no open spaces next to her truck, then walked toward the entrance of the farm. A busload of kids had been gathered together and split into two groups, one led by Hailey, the other led by a short rather wiry woman in her midfifties who he assumed was Nora Rhodes.

Watching Hailey in action was interesting. She clearly had a way of getting the kids' attention, which surprised him as she'd been so quiet during their time together. He hung back out of view so he could watch without drawing her attention. He noticed she'd somehow changed her clothes from the hiking shorts and tank top she'd been wearing to a pair of jeans and a polo shirt with the hobby farm logo on it. Either Nora had spare items here or they'd been in her truck.

Hailey's loud clear voice described the different animals they'd see, then went over the rules, which included no pinching, kicking, or hitting people or animals. He had to smile when she aimed a few direct glares at some of the boys who were already pushing and shoving each other in a way that indicated they might cause trouble.

"Okay, are you ready to feed the goats?" she asked.

"Yeah!" the group of kids shouted.

"Follow me and keep your buddy close," she warned. As Hailey led her group of kids lined up in pairs toward the goat pen, he realized there was no way on earth she would leave in the middle of a bus tour.

Especially since this was obviously why she'd come in the first place. To assist with the group of kids. Easy to see Nora would have struggled to manage them by herself.

He decided against fighting that uphill battle. Probably better for him to head home. He could shower and change, then return with lunch. Surely Nora wouldn't mind if Hailey took a midday break.

Especially since he knew Hailey hadn't had anything more than a power bar for dinner last night and breakfast this morning.

He turned and headed back toward the parking lot. As he headed past Hailey's truck on the way to his SUV, he frowned. Her rusted Chevy was sitting on four flat tires. Moving closer and kneeling on the gravel, he noticed the shredded rubber obviously had been created by several slashes of a large knife.

The same knife that had been used to wreak havoc on the interior of her trailer? Most likely.

He swept his gaze over the area, searching for a possible suspect lurking nearby.

He didn't see anyone, but that didn't mean someone wasn't out there, hiding and watching.

Waiting for the next moment to strike.

# CHAPTER FIVE

Hailey kept a keen eye on the group of twelve kids who were under her care while touring the hobby farm. There were two boys who seemed to be possible sources of trouble, but so far, they'd managed to behave.

Not that she expected that to last the entire morning.

Her stomach rumbled with hunger to the point even the goat pellets looked tasty. Thankfully, Nora had coffee on when she'd arrived, which had helped keep her exhaustion at bay.

Normally she brought a bag lunch, simply because it was cheaper than buying food from the café. Leaving her trailer so abruptly the way she had meant she didn't have much cash on her. Maybe three bucks? Pathetic. Hopefully, Darby, if she was the one who'd trashed her trailer, hadn't found her secret stash of cash hidden in the freezer.

If she had, paying her July rent would be tricky.

"The baby goat bit me," one little girl said with a sob.

"Let me see." Hailey went over to examine the little girl's hand. There were no obvious teeth marks, no blood, not even a hint of broken skin. She smiled reassuringly.

"You're fine, maybe the goat was a little overexcited." She knelt beside the child. "What's your name?"

"Maribelle," the little girl said with a sniff.

"Okay, Maribelle. Come stand next to me, okay?" Hailey rose and took the little girl by the hand. "We'll be finishing up here soon."

"Okay," Maribelle agreed. The kid reminded her of Caitlin, who'd been nine when they'd escaped the Preacher.

She wondered where Jayme and Caitlin were now? Hopefully doing better with acclimating to life than she was.

Glancing over, she checked on Nora. Her boss's group of kids were just about finished with their pony rides. She and Nora had the day-care kids tour down to a manageable routine. One group fed goats while the other group rode ponies, then they swapped. After that, they each went to pet the donkeys and llamas, before packing the kids back into their bus to head back.

The afternoon tours would arrive around one o'clock, and they'd do the same thing all over again. When the last bus left for the day, she and Nora typically split up the job of caring for the animals, although as the owner, Nora tended to do more of that work.

Since Hailey had been late today, she figured she should stay later to make up for it. It would be good for Nora to have a chance to leave early. Nora's life was almost as boring as hers.

Remembering how her leaving early had led to a nearly fatal hike made her grimace. Hailey would have been better off staying to help Nora. That way, she might have caught Darby in the act of trashing her trailer.

There wasn't time to think about where she should start searching for her foster sister now. She glanced around, noting that all the goat food pellets were pretty much gone. "Okay, kids, I need you to get back in your buddy lines. We're going over to the ponies, and if you'd like to have a ride, we'll walk you around the paddock."

"Can I ride the pony?" Maribelle asked, her apparent goat-bitten hand forgotten. "Please?"

"Sure, you can. Now find your buddy." Hailey registered movement from the corner of her eye and turned to see Rock striding toward her, his expression grim. She lifted a hand as if to make him back off. "I'm sorry, Rock, but I'm working."

"Your truck has been vandalized," he said bluntly.

"What? When?" she demanded.

"Between the time I arrived here and now," he said, looking at his phone. "Maybe forty-five minutes?"

Forty-five minutes? "You've been here all this time?"

"Hailey, focus," Rock said sternly. "I'm telling you, all four of your truck tires have been slashed with a knife. I checked the area around the truck but didn't see anyone lurking nearby."

Slashed with a knife. The image of her ruined belongings in the trailer flashed in her mind. Whoever had done that damage had also used a knife.

First gunshots aimed at her, now a knife used to slash her things. What was next? She didn't really want to know.

"Do you want me to call Morrison?" Rock asked, looking at her with frustration. "These acts of violence are escalating, you really can't keep ignoring them."

Yes, she could ignore them, especially if Darby was the culprit.

But Rock obviously couldn't.

"You can call him, but as you can see, I'm working. I won't have time to discuss it until I'm finished."

"Hailey, what is wrong with you? It's like you don't even care that everything you own is being destroyed."

"I care," she retorted hotly. "But what would you like me to do, Rock? If I don't work, I can't earn the money I need to fix things." And not having her truck would be a huge problem, one with ramifications she didn't want to think about at the moment.

"Hailey—" he began, but Nora cut him off.

"What's going on?" Nora glanced from Rock to Hailey. "Is there a problem here?"

Hailey inwardly groaned. This wasn't the time or the place to discuss her issues, especially since she hadn't told Nora about finding the damage to her trailer. She'd only mentioned gunfire in the mountains but downplayed the event by saying it may have been nothing more than a poacher. "Park Ranger Wilson was just telling me that the tires on my truck have been slashed."

"What? That's terrible." Nora looked shocked and disturbed, which was exactly what Hailey had been afraid of. "If you need to leave, I can handle the kids by myself."

"No, it's a two-man job." And the hobby farm was Nora's livelihood. She turned back to Rock, warning him with a narrow glare not to say too much. "I'll call Officer Morrison on my lunch break at noon, okay? I have things to do until then."

Rock did not look the least bit happy, but thankfully he didn't argue. She herded her group of kids over to the pony rides and lifted the first four kids onto their respective ponies to lead them around the ring.

But as she worked, her mind whirled. All of this stuff, shooting at her, wrecking her trailer, and slashing her tires, seemed over the top, even for Darby. Granted, the screaming match they'd had the last time they were together had been awful. Hailey had never seen her sister as furious as she'd been when Hailey had tried to intervene in Darby's relationship with Aaron, who she suspected was dealing drugs. But to go to this extent?

It honestly didn't make much sense.

And if not Darby, then who? She hadn't seen any of the other fosters since disappearing into the mountains after the fire.

These attacks were personal. And only Darby had a reason to lash out at her. Not a good reason, but who knows what had happened in the time they'd been apart?

Rock was right about one thing, the attacks against her were escalating. If Rock hadn't been here to find the slashed tires, it would have been late in the day before she'd noticed.

She couldn't help wondering what the attacker's plan had been. To wait and hide, coming out to strike in the deserted parking lot after everyone was gone?

Despite the heat of the sun, she shivered.

Her cavalier attitude was a charade. Deep down, she knew she didn't want to die. Self-preservation had gotten her through the years in the Preacher's cabin and had carried her to where she was now.

Yet she wasn't sure what to do. If Nora knew that someone had targeted Hailey specifically, rather than some random act, her boss might not want her to work at the hobby farm. Was her presence here at the hobby farm exposing the kids to danger?

Slashed tires made it seem like the plan was to come after her specifically, and no one else. Yet could she really risk a child's life?

No, she couldn't.

In fact, protecting Darby was what had gotten her into trouble with the law back when she was seventeen. Stealing so she could feed her younger sister, hoping to relocate to a new place where they could get decent jobs. A plan that had backfired since Darby had screamed that she'd rather stay with Aaron than with Hailey.

Old news, or so she thought. Unless something had happened to cause Darby to come after her at this point in time. Like maybe Darby had been arrested too. The idea was sobering. As she swapped out kids on ponies with robotic motions, she grimly realized that her initial instinct of leaving town might have been right on target.

Even though she didn't want to start over in a new place, find a new job and a new place to live, it seemed she might not have an option. If her presence here at the farm was putting the kids at risk of being harmed, she couldn't stay.

No matter how much she wanted to.

It was a sad testament to the state of her future. She'd come so far in the past thirteen years.

Yet not far enough.

It seemed that no matter what she did in an effort to lead a normal life, there was no way to escape the chains of her past.

All because of the Preacher.

---

ROCK STALKED AWAY from Hailey and the kids, inwardly fuming at her incredible stubborn streak. He considered calling Morrison himself but decided to take the time he had to head home to shower and change. He'd hesitated, then decided to put on another uniform, since he wanted Hailey to remember he was a member of law enforcement. Additionally, he wanted to remain armed.

Bringing lunch while Hailey spoke to Morrison was likely his best option to get her cooperation.

Using his phone, he'd taken a picture of her truck's slashed tires. He should have done the same at her trailer, determined to include both incidents with his report about the gunfire.

Morrison might not be a crooked cop, but Rock didn't think he was the sharpest knife in the drawer. More lazy than incompetent.

At least Hailey had been working during the time her tires had been slashed. Even a jerk like Morrison had to agree that she couldn't have done the damage herself.

Rock left his cabin, then noticed the road leading to the Whispering Oaks Trailer Park. At the last minute, he cranked the steering wheel to the left to head toward Hailey's place. By now the crime scene team should have been there, but the area in front of trailer number thirteen was vacant.

Reining in a harsh thought toward Morrison, Rock threw the gearshift of his SUV into park and shut down the engine. Taking his phone from the car charger, he approached Hailey's home.

From the doorway, he took several photos of the interior destruction. While he didn't want to destroy any evidence, he wanted to see if there was some clue Morrison had overlooked.

The shredded sofa cushions, the clothing ripped and tossed around reinforced his belief that this attack was personal. Someone harbored a deep hatred of Hailey and certainly wanted her to know it.

He found a small disposable phone that had been smashed into tiny pieces by either a hammer or a bootheel.

Rock leaned toward the latter because most of the destruction had clearly been done by a knife.

It didn't take long for him to work his way through the small trailer. He stood in the center of the living area with a frown.

There wasn't a single personal photograph that he could see. Not of Hailey as a baby, her parents, or siblings. It struck him as odd, although he supposed it was possible the attacker had taken them.

No, that didn't make sense. Because Hailey would have noticed and likely have said something if photographs were missing. Maybe not, he was forced to amend. During their time together on the mountain, she'd been closemouthed about her personal life, other than mentioning her ex-boyfriend, Jacob Rokeby, who'd left her for another woman, and needing to call Nora to let her know she'd be in late for work.

Kids didn't spring out of nowhere, but that's the impression Hailey had given. She was independent and a loner who knew how to survive in the wilderness. And if he hadn't been close enough to respond to the gunfire, he knew full well she would have gotten herself safely off the mountain to face the trashed trailer on her own.

And he'd bet his last paycheck she wouldn't have called the police either.

Rock left the Whispering Oaks Trailer Park, his thoughts whirling. He'd spent more time at Hailey's trailer than he'd realized and still had more questions than answers.

He drove until he found a fast-food restaurant. He purchased burgers and fries for himself, Hailey, and Nora, before returning to the hobby farm.

He could see Hailey's group of kids petting the donkeys

and wondered if any of the kids were causing problems. For a loner, he found it interesting that Hailey appeared to establish a rapport with the kids.

The hour was close to eleven thirty, early for lunch, but he couldn't shake the feeling that he needed to be there to force the issue of her reporting the truck damage to the police.

"Okay, let's head inside to use the bathrooms," Hailey called in a loud, clear voice. "Get in your buddy lines and follow me."

The building appeared to have dual purposes of functioning as the office and farm headquarters to the team working there and as a gift shop open to the public. He followed Hailey's line of kids inside. If she noticed him, she didn't let on.

"I smell fries," one of the kids said. "I'm hungry!"

"You'll be getting lunch back at the day care," Hailey assured them as she stood like a sentinel between the two bathrooms. "Go now or wait until you get back to the day care," she advised.

Most of the kids crowded into the restrooms. Hailey finally met his gaze. "Take the bag of food to the office, these kids might start a riot over those french fries." She frowned. "You should know better than to bring that anywhere near a group of perpetually hungry kids."

"Yes, ma'am," he said. "Sorry to cause trouble, although I brought enough food for you, me, and Nora."

Her stomach let out a rumbling noise that was so loud he could hear it from where he stood. Hailey blushed and nodded. "Fine." Then she added, "Thanks."

"You're welcome. I'm starving too." He shot her a quick grin, then veered through the building toward the office area. There was a round table in the corner of the room, so he sat down and unpacked the meals he'd purchased.

After fifteen minutes of getting the kids gathered around outside and filed onto the bus, both Hailey and Nora joined him.

"Thank you for lunch," Nora said with a smile.

Hailey nodded in agreement but had already taken a bite of burger. He didn't blame her and didn't waste a moment diving into his meal either.

For a long moment there was nothing but silence as they ate.

"Did you call Morrison?" Rock asked between bites.

Hailey shook her head, sending a furtive glance at Nora. "I don't have my cell phone."

"Use the office phone, Hailey." Nora waved a hand toward it. Through the open door, he could see a small black landline phone on the desk. "I can't believe someone vandalized your truck. You don't think it was Owen, do you?"

It took a moment for Rock to remember Owen was the kid who'd pinched the donkey. He shook his head. "I don't think so, unless he has access to a very large knife."

Nora's brow furrowed with concern. "I don't like the sound of that," she murmured.

"I'll call Morrison now." Hailey abruptly stood and crossed over to the desk. He jumped up to join her.

"You'll need this." He handed her Morrison's business card.

"Thanks." She avoided his gaze as she made the call. "Officer Morrison? This is Hailey Donovan. I'm at the Rhodes Hobby Farm, and my truck tires have been slashed. Park Ranger Wilson thought you should know."

Rock wanted to roll his eyes at her last statement. It was

clear she'd made the call under duress. He watched her expression, but her features remained impassive.

"I'll be here for the rest of the afternoon. Our last tour leaves around four o'clock, so I can talk to you then, okay? Bye." She replaced the receiver and looked at him. "Happy?"

"For now," he admitted. "Thanks for making the call."

"Thanks for lunch," she replied politely in return.

"Are you really going to stay here at work all afternoon?"

She looked surprised by his question. "We have another tour bus coming at one, so yes, I'll be here."

"Okay, then I'm going to head home for a bit, but I'll meet you back here at four o'clock, okay? I figure it's better for Morrison if I'm here when he interviews you."

A ghost of a smile played across her features. "Probably. I don't care for him much."

"Yeah, you don't have a very good poker face."

They returned to their respective seats at the table and finished their food. No surprise that Hailey finished first. She jumped up from her seat and excused herself. She disappeared in the direction of the restrooms.

Nora eyed him curiously after Hailey was gone. "Is she in trouble?"

He hesitated, unsure how to respond. Especially since he was fairly certain she hadn't told Nora about the destruction of her trailer. "I'm afraid so," he finally admitted. "Has she said anything to you about someone carrying a grudge against her?"

"Not a word," Nora said.

"Well, keep a close eye out for anyone lurking around," Rock advised.

"I'm worried about her," Nora said in a low voice. "She

doesn't have any friends that I'm aware of, but the slashed tires indicate she must have made an enemy along the way."

Before Nora could say anything more, Hailey returned, eyeing them suspiciously as if sensing they'd been talking about her. "I'm going to rotate the goats before our next bus," she said to Nora.

"Rotate the goats?" he echoed. They weren't car tires, were they?

"They don't eat all day," Hailey explained. "The afternoon kids feed a different group of goats than those from the morning session."

"I see." Rock stood and gathered their discarded wrappers together. "I'd better leave you to it, then. I'll see you later, Hailey."

"Yeah, sure." Her response was less than enthusiastic.

He was almost all the way back to his SUV when he heard a female voice call out, "Ranger Wilson?"

He turned to find Nora rushing toward him. "What is it?"

"I don't think you should leave," Nora said bluntly. "I care about Hailey like a daughter, but she's been remote and distant all morning. Not that she was ever a chatterbox, but she seems more withdrawn than usual."

"What has she told you about her past?" Rock asked, squelching the flash of guilt at prying into Hailey's background.

It was Nora's turn to hesitate. "Nothing really, although she did mention she'd spent time in jail when she was younger."

"She did?" It surprised him that Hailey had mentioned her stint in juvie. "Did she tell you what happened?"

"Not in so many words, but I had the sense she was a runaway and had fallen on tough times as a result." Nora shrugged and waved a hand. "There's nothing glamorous about working with the animals, but Hailey acted as if I'd given her a diamond ring when I offered her the job. I had the sense others were put off by her juvie record. Despite that, she's been the hardest and most dependable worker I've ever employed. My business has grown these past five years, and I'm convinced she's the reason why."

"I'm sure she's an honorable person," Rock agreed. "She was truly concerned about being late for work this morning."

"I'd never be upset at her for being late for work," Nora protested. "She should know me better than that."

"I'm sure she does, but she also doesn't want to disappoint you." He hesitated, then added, "She isn't going anywhere, her truck isn't drivable."

"We have an old truck here at the farm, and Hailey has a key." Nora's gaze brimmed with concern. "I'm afraid if you leave, she'll find a way to disappear, forever."

## CHAPTER SIX

Hailey had trouble concentrating on the task of moving the second group of goats from the indoor pen to the outdoor pen, preoccupied with planning her escape from Gatlinburg. Each option she came up with was ruthlessly rejected, until she realized she was being too picky.

Mainly because she didn't really want to leave.

But she didn't see an alternative. Running was what had kept her safe after escaping the Preacher. And now she needed to keep Nora and the kids safe too. Which left her two viable options, basically steal Nora's truck or hike through the mountains.

She could probably scrape together enough provisions from her trailer to hike. If her backpack hadn't been damaged too badly. And her tent too. There was also the remote possibility the intruder hadn't found her secret stash of cash. With that money, she could hitch a ride into town and find a taxi to get out of Gatlinburg.

The taxi would be expensive, but once she was in Knoxville, she could get on a bus. No matter how much easier it would be to have a set of wheels, she couldn't bring herself to steal Nora's truck. Especially since she'd be leaving her useless Chevy sans wheels in exchange.

Hailey barely had the goats situated when the school bus pulled in. Drumming up enthusiasm for the tour wasn't easy, but she put her game face on and approached the bus.

Nora quickly joined her. "All set?" her boss asked with forced cheerfulness.

"Yeah." Hailey frowned, noting the shadow of concern in Nora's gaze.

As the kids filed off the bus, they split them into groups. Hailey took the lead, going over the rules in a loud clear voice, reciting the speech from memory.

A hint of movement off to the side caught her attention. For a long moment, her heart froze in her chest. Then she recognized Rock leaning against the side of the office building, his arms crossed over his chest.

She let out her breath in a soundless whoosh. Then scowled. Why was Rock sticking around? She glanced at Nora who avoided her gaze by appearing to be engrossed in counting the kids in her group.

She bristled at Rock taking on the role of her protector, maybe even her babysitter. She'd called that jerk Morrison, hadn't she? What more did he want from her?

The afternoon tour dragged on with incredible slowness. Rock disappeared soon after she'd taken her group of kids to feed the goats, which helped her relax a bit. She didn't appreciate being scrutinized by the ranger.

Coming to the hobby farm seemed like something your average park ranger wouldn't do. Didn't he have poachers to catch? Lost hikers to find? Surely the summer tourist season kept the rangers busy.

It didn't sit well that Rock might be putting his job on

the line to help her. Especially since she didn't need his help.

Not when her ultimate goal was to get out of Dodge.

"Hey, no hitting the llamas," she said in a sharp tone. The little girl who'd slapped at Lucy put her hands on her hips in defiance.

"It spit at me!"

"Lucy is a baby llama, she doesn't know any better. You don't hit babies, do you?" Hailey could feel her temper fraying and fought to keep a smile on her face. "Come away from Lucy, I'm sure she's tired of all the attention."

"She shouldn't spit at us," the little girl muttered. Hailey tried to remember the girl's name but couldn't. Normally, she prided herself on paying attention to detail, keeping the kids' names straight, but not today.

Finally, the school bus returned to pick up the kids. Hailey had never been so relieved to finish a tour. Avoiding Nora, she headed straight over to feed the llamas. Then she began to muck out their pen.

Morrison would arrive any minute. She dreaded talking to the patronizing cop, but she'd promised Rock. At the time, calling him in exchange for lunch seemed like a good deal.

Whatever. She'd answer Morrison's questions and then find a way to get back to her trailer. Hopefully, Nora would give her a ride.

"Hailey?" Rock's low voice startled her so badly she dropped the pitchfork.

"You shouldn't sneak up on me," she snapped.

He lifted a brow. "Sorry, I thought you heard me. Officer Morrison is here to take your statement."

"Okay, I'm almost finished." Stubbornly, she picked up

the pitchfork and completed her task of placing fresh straw in the pen, then carried the pitchfork back to the toolshed.

Rock walked with her as if she couldn't be trusted to show up on her own. She tried not to be cranky, but her lack of sleep was catching up to her. He'd showered and changed into a fresh uniform, something she hadn't been able to do.

She shook off the annoyance and slowed when she saw Morrison standing next to her rusted Chevy. "Ms. Donovan," he said. "Looks like someone is pretty upset with you."

"And as I told you and Ranger Wilson earlier, I have no idea who is behind these attacks." She fought to keep her tone even.

She heard a snorting sound coming from Rock but studiously ignored him, keeping her gaze on Morrison.

"Well now, that's hard to believe since these attacks appear to be personal," Morrison drawled. "We haven't seen any other random acts of vandalism in the area."

"I agree they're personal," she admitted. "My last boyfriend was a guy named Jacob Rokeby. He left me, but maybe he's angry about something I did that I'm not aware of." It was a lame suggestion, but it was all she could offer.

Morrison made a show of writing Jacob's name in his notebook. "What about someone from your past?"

His question caught her off guard, and for a split second, she wondered how he'd found out about the Preacher. Then it dawned on her that Morrison had run a background check on her.

"My juvenile record has nothing to do with this," she said, avoiding Rock's all-too-knowing hazel gaze. "That was over ten years ago now. No reason anyone would come back to exact revenge at this point."

"Not even someone you served time with?" Morrison pressed.

"No." She curled her fingers into fists in an effort to control her anger. This was exactly why she hadn't wanted to get law enforcement involved. Morrison was useless. It was clear he was of the opinion that once a criminal, always a criminal.

Her court-appointed lawyer had promised her juvie record would remain sealed. Had Morrison found a judge willing to unseal the file? Or was he just egging her on?

Suspecting the latter, she lifted her chin and stared him down. He'd never escaped an abusive foster home situation and struggled to find food while supporting a younger sister. Yeah, she'd stolen to support herself and Darby.

Under the same set of circumstances, she'd do it again.

"We're just looking at any possibilities, Hailey," Rock said, breaking the silence.

"And I already told you, I don't know who is responsible for this." She might suspect Darby, but she wasn't about to throw her foster sibling under the bus. Not until she knew for sure. "I left work at four thirty, returned to my trailer, and decided to go for a short hike. My trailer was fine when I left. While I was on the trail, someone shot at me. I hit the ground, and when a second shot followed, I hid in the brush. I was there when Ranger Wilson came up to see what had happened. A third shot forced us to abandon the trail. We found an abandoned cabin to spend the night. We came down the Beaver Trail this morning, and that's when I found my trailer had been trashed. I left you, came to work, and didn't see anyone near my truck. Rock is the one who told me the tires had been slashed. He asked me to report the vandalism to you, so I did." She reiterated the events in a dispassionate tone. "That's all I know. Now if you'll both excuse me, I need to finish caring for the animals."

Without waiting for a response, she turned and walked away, anger simmering beneath the surface.

How dare Morrison embarrass her by bringing up her juvie record? The jerk just had to get that information out there, didn't he?

"Hailey, wait." Rock's voice came from behind her, but she didn't turn to look at him. She needed some time with the animals.

"Hailey, I'm only going to wait until you're finished," Rock said in a warning tone.

"Go ahead." She didn't care how he spent his time. "Although I'm surprised you don't have better things to do."

"I'm already in trouble with my boss, so it doesn't matter."

Rock's comment made her hesitate. "I didn't ask you to stay."

"I know, but you'll need a ride back to your trailer, right? And some help getting the place cleaned up."

Somehow, his kind offer punched a hole through her balloon of anger. She turned to face him. "Is Morrison gone?"

"Yeah." Rock rubbed the back of his neck. "Look, I know the guy is a jerk, but I still believe it's important to get these vandalism incidents on record in a police report."

It would be important if she was planning to stick around, but she wasn't. No sense arguing. "I have to take care of the donkeys before I can leave."

"Like I said, I'll wait." There was no denying the flash of relief in his gaze.

She turned and headed into the donkey stable. Why Rock was being so nice was a mystery, but she couldn't afford to turn down his offer of a ride. It was one less thing for her to worry about.

Once he'd taken her to the trailer park, she'd find a way to get rid of him. There was no sense in cleaning up the mess in the trailer.

She didn't plan to sleep there. Instead, she'd be gone before nightfall.

---

ROCK HAD GOTTEN SO angry with Morrison that it was either walk away or say something he'd regret.

The cop had brought up Hailey's criminal past on purpose, just to make her feel like a loser. Whatever she'd done as a juvenile couldn't have been that bad, or she'd still be locked up somewhere. Knowing what he did about her, a woman with her work ethic and compassion for animals she couldn't have done anything too terrible.

Likely shoplifting or underage drinking or marijuana possession. Typical teenage trouble. And certainly not linked to someone shooting at her.

Hailey's response of going pale, then flushing with embarrassment had made Rock feel terrible for his unwitting role in the whole thing.

No wonder Hailey hadn't wanted law enforcement involved. If all her interactions had been with guys like Morrison, he could understand why she had no use for them.

His cell phone battery had died again, and he dreaded recharging it, knowing there'd be several messages from his boss.

Rock didn't think he'd get fired over this, but he'd end up working the less desirable shifts for the remainder of the summer, that was for sure.

A decision he could live with. For some reason, Hailey's

predicament bothered him. Her nightmare indicated she'd suffered along the way, and he couldn't bear the idea of leaving her to fend for herself.

Granted, becoming emotionally involved with her would be a huge mistake.

One he didn't dare make.

He waited patiently for Hailey to finish with the donkeys, smiling a bit as she jutted sideways to avoid a kick. When she finished, she came over to where he stood. "I need to talk to Nora."

"Okay." He followed her back to the office area, where Nora was working on a pile of paperwork. She looked up in surprise to see them in the doorway.

"Oh, I thought you'd left," Nora said.

"I finished with the donkey barn and the llama pens," Hailey informed her. "Is there anything else you need before I go?"

"No, but thanks." Nora darted a gaze at Rock before smiling at Hailey. "I appreciate everything you've done, Hailey. We don't have a morning tour tomorrow, so if you'd like to sleep in, that's fine."

"Ah, okay. Thanks." Was it his imagination or did a flash of guilt cross Hailey's features? "Take care, Nora." Hailey turned away.

"Hailey?" Nora called, stopping her. Hailey glanced at her. "I couldn't do this without your help, so thanks again for coming in today, despite your rough night."

Hailey frowned and nodded. "I enjoy working with the animals, Nora. And with you too. Good night."

"Good night," Nora said, her stricken gaze following Hailey's retreating form. She looked at Rock expectantly.

"I know, and I'll do my best," he assured Nora, understanding her fear that her best employee was going to disappear, never to be seen again. He rushed to catch up to Hailey, relieved to find her waiting beside his SUV.

He unlocked the vehicle with his key fob, and she quickly slid in. She seemed grateful for the ride but was quiet as he hit the highway leading to the Whispering Oaks Trailer Park.

"Nora has a really great business going, doesn't she?" He glanced at Hailey, hoping to draw her into a conversation.

"Yeah." Instead of saying anything more, Hailey turned to stare out the passenger-side window. At that moment, he knew Nora's fears were dead-on. Hailey was already distancing herself from the hobby farm.

"Hailey, I really want to help you," he said as the entrance for the trailer park came into view. "Won't you please let me?"

There was a momentary silence before she spoke. "I appreciate your offer, Rock. But there isn't anything you can do. I'll be fine."

He blew out a frustrated breath as he pulled into the empty parking spot next to trailer number thirteen. "It's obvious to anyone with eyes in their head that you're used to handling things on your own. But you don't have to. I can help investigate who is behind the vandalism and the gunfire." He paused, then added, "Unless you really don't want that person to be found."

He knew he'd struck a nerve when she glanced at him in shock, before looking quickly away. "You heard Officer Morrison, I have a checkered past."

"He was a huge jerk for bringing that up." He didn't hide his disgust. "I find it hard to believe some juvie stint resulted in someone taking shots at you, Hailey. But I also know you're not being honest with me."

She sighed. "My stint in juvie was no big deal. I was only held for thirty days, then did some community service."

Exactly what he'd thought. "So your checkered past isn't really about the time you spent in the system."

Again, her slight flinch indicated he'd hit a sore spot. Then she pushed open the door and jumped out. "Goodbye, Rock. Thanks for your help." She slammed the door and headed inside the trailer.

Most people would take the giant hint and leave her alone. But he wasn't going to give up that easily. He threw open his door and quickly followed her inside.

Hailey had gone straight to the kitchen and was rooting around in the freezer. He noticed she stuffed something in her pocket and for a moment wondered if he'd been wrong about her.

Drugs? Was it possible she was involved in something criminal after all?

Before he could stop himself, he strode over and grabbed her hand. "What did you put in your pocket?"

She narrowed her eyes. "None of your business."

"I'm a peace officer, so yeah, it is." He tightened his grip. "Especially if it's drugs."

To his surprise, she rolled her eyes. "Drugs? You must be joking." She pulled at her pocket, and he saw a wad of low-denomination bills. "If you must know, I keep my cash in a box in the freezer. Thankfully, the person who trashed the place didn't find it."

"Cash?" He flushed, feeling stupid. "Don't trust banks?"

"Not really." She shook off his hand and stepped away. "Now if you don't mind, I'd like you to leave. I need to get some sleep."

Sleep? In this mess? Yeah, he wasn't buying that line. "I'll help you clean up."

"No." Her sharp tone held a note of finality. "It's my place, I'll handle it. Look, I'm tired and crabby. Don't take this the wrong way, but I'd like you to leave."

Sensing she wasn't going to change her mind, he gave in. "Fine. But if you need a ride to the hobby farm tomorrow, I'd be happy to take you."

"Thanks, but I don't have a phone." Hailey shrugged. "It's only two miles, I can walk. I've done it before."

He believed her. Hailey was the most stubborn woman he'd ever met. With reluctance, he turned and left the trailer. Feeling as if he'd let Nora down, he climbed into his SUV and drove out of the trailer park.

But then he pulled off onto the side of the road. Maybe Hailey would stay in the trailer overnight and leave come morning. Or maybe she'd hit the road tonight.

Not that he wanted to sleep in the car. Bone-weary exhaustion weighed him down, and if he had half a brain, he'd leave Hailey alone. She wasn't a kid, she was old enough to make her own decisions. If she wanted to leave town, she could. There was no law against it.

It bugged him that she wouldn't open up as to who she suspected might be responsible for the shooting and vandalism, but getting her to talk proved more difficult than convincing a llama to stop spitting.

He rested his wrist on the steering wheel, watching the road. Rock told himself he'd give her twenty minutes, then he was done. She wasn't the only one who was tired and crabby.

At the twenty-minute mark, he started the SUV, knowing it was past time for him to get home. He'd charged his phone and had several upset messages from his boss. Tomorrow would be spent smoothing things over.

And for what? A woman with the same personality as Rory the kicking donkey.

He gaped as Hailey walked from the trailer park road onto the highway. She had a large russet backpack on her shoulders, no doubt packed full of whatever personal items she'd been able to salvage from the wreckage of her trailer.

God must be telling him something. Rock put the SUV in gear and turned around to pull up beside her. She glanced at him in horror, but in a moment, her expression turned neutral.

"Get in." He wasn't in the mood to take no for an answer.

She shook her head and kept walking. He eased forward, easily keeping pace.

"Hailey, I mean it. Get in. If you need a ride somewhere, I'll take you."

"No." Her dismissal rankled, but before he could say anything more, a shot rang out. He instinctively ducked in his seat, braced for another bullet to follow, this one hitting his SUV.

"GET IN!" he shouted.

The gunfire must have shaken her because Hailey quickly shrugged out of her pack, tossed it over the passenger seat, and climbed in. Without hesitation, he hit the gas and roared down the highway as far from the gunfire as possible.

As he drove, Rock grimly realized that if he hadn't waited for Hailey, she would likely have been killed right there at the side of the highway.

## CHAPTER SEVEN

Her flare of annoyance at Rock pulling up beside her vanished in the wake of more gunfire. A wave of bitter fear hit hard.

Why? After all she'd been through, why was this happening to her? This, along with the crazed ranting of the Preacher, is what convinced her there was no God.

If there was a higher power, she'd be tempted to pray. But hadn't she and the other kids spent useless hours on their knees praying? And for what? To be treated like animals.

Worse than animals.

Tears pricked at her eyes as her heart thundered in her chest.

"Are you okay?" Rock's rough tone penetrated her tumultuous thoughts. "You didn't get hit, did you?"

"No." Although she'd felt something whizz past her ear. Close. Far too close. She put her hand up to feel along her hairline, but she didn't find any blood. She licked her dry lips. "Thanks for rescuing me, again."

"You could have died back there!" His rare spurt of

anger caught her off guard. She reared back in shock as he continued, "Don't you see? You can't run from this."

"How do you know?" she shot back. "Do you think I want to be a target for some maniac with a knife and a gun? I have to leave in order to protect Nora and the kids!" When she realized she was shouting, she took a breath and lowered her voice, doing her best to maintain some semblance of control. "If you could take me to the trolley station, I'd appreciate it."

"Yeah, no. Don't think so." Rock's hands were tight on the steering wheel.

"I mean it," she insisted. "You can drop me off and never look back. Can't you see that sticking with me is dangerous?"

"Yeah, no lie," he said dryly. "Which is why we're going someplace safe for what's left of the night. We can come up with a new plan in the morning."

Despite her fear and exhaustion, she stiffened. "I'm not spending the night with you."

He turned to look at her incredulously. "Really? After everything that's happened, you honestly believe I'd take advantage of the situation by coming on to you? Wow, I guess you don't think much of me, do you?"

She closed her eyes, feeling guilty over her knee-jerk reaction. Of course, she didn't think he'd take advantage of her. Rock had been nothing but kind, and they'd already spent the night together in an abandoned cabin without him so much as hinting at crossing the line. Hadn't she admitted to herself that she trusted him? "I'm sorry."

"You should be." He bypassed the hobby farm, heading into downtown Gatlinburg. "I would never hurt you, Hailey. We'll stay in a hotel, platonically," he added with emphasis. "My cabin is farther up the highway past your trailer park, and I'm not about to head in the direction where the gunfire came from. For all we know, the shooter is still in the area." He frowned, then added, "The same general direction the initial gunfire came from, now that I think about it."

"Yeah, okay." She didn't have the energy to fight him any longer. Truthfully, she was grateful for the lift. She'd told herself the hike into town wouldn't be that bad, but now that she was sitting in Rock's SUV, a wave of sheer exhaustion washed over her.

*She really was getting soft*, she thought with disgust.

Glancing at Rock, she noted his set jaw and somber features. The man had gone out of his way more than once to help her out of a tough spot. And what had he gotten in return? Nothing.

Not that he wanted anything other than gratitude. Which only made her trust him more.

Deep down, though, she knew she couldn't stay with Rock for long. Being dependent on anyone, much less a man, wasn't her style. Unfortunately, she liked Rock, more than she should. An unexpected physical attraction that was completely one-sided. Yet she also knew that Rock wasn't the kind of guy to let her take off for parts unknown without an argument.

He'd encourage her to stay and fight the nameless and faceless enemy.

And there was a part of her that wanted to do just that.

Even if that meant fighting her foster sister.

Only she could not, would not put Nora and the kids in danger. That was nonnegotiable. It was difficult enough for her to leave the only real home she'd had. The safe haven she'd craved long before she'd ended up in the Preacher's cabin. Having Rock argue with her made sticking to her decision ten times harder.

"Do you really think Nora and the kids are in danger?" Rock asked, breaking the silence.

"Don't you?" She winced at the sarcasm and smoothed out her tone. "Come on, Rock. You know as well as I do I can't stay here. Not when someone clearly has it out for me. What if the next gunfire comes when I'm at the farm, talking to the kids?" The very thought made her feel sick to her stomach. She turned in her seat to face him. "I couldn't live with myself if something happened to an innocent child. Or any of the animals," she added.

He didn't answer, but she sensed he finally understood why she'd set out on her own. She glanced in the back seat at her backpack. The intruder had slashed it, but duct tape worked wonders, and she felt certain it would hold long enough for her to get settled in some new location.

Where? She had no idea. At the moment, she couldn't come up with a destination that interested her in the least.

Her thoughts returned to the recent gunfire she'd barely escaped. Who'd taken the shot at her? Darby? The escalation of the attacks made it hard to believe Darby was behind them. Maybe Darby might have been angry enough to trash her trailer and slash her tires, but this constant shooting?

It was difficult to comprehend.

One of the boys, then? Sawyer, Cooper, or Trent? But if so, why? They'd all escaped the Preacher's root cellar and certain death at the same time, so why would one of them hold a grudge against her?

Especially thirteen years after the fact?

Her head throbbed, and her stomach rolled at the thought of any of the foster kids attacking her so viciously.

"Are you hungry?" Rock asked.

"Not really." Then she felt bad, thinking of how Rock was likely hungry. Their lunch seemed like hours ago. "Well, I can probably eat," she amended. She patted the roll of bills in her pocket. Finding her secret stash of cash undisturbed had been the bright spot of her evening. "I can pay for dinner."

He sighed and muttered something incomprehensible beneath his breath. He gestured to several fast-food restaurants lining the street. "I was thinking we should get something other than burgers. Chicken? Tacos? What would you prefer?"

"A bucket of chicken would be great," she said, a hint of longing in her tone. Now that she'd thought about eating, she became aware of a gnawing hunger. Likely the spike of adrenaline after being shot at. "I don't usually eat this much fast food, but I'm hungry enough to eat a bear."

"Bear isn't as good as you'd think," he said wryly.

"You hunt?" she asked in surprise. She wouldn't have expected Rock to be the type to shoot wild game.

"No, but we had to put a wounded bear down, thanks to some idiot poacher who'd left him wounded and very mad. My boss decided we should eat the animal rather than waste the meat." He wrinkled his nose. "It wasn't very good, despite the way my boss raved about it."

She nodded, thinking of the small game she'd hunted and lived off of while hiding in the woods. Rabbit was her favorite, followed by venison. She'd never eaten bear but didn't doubt the large animal would have a strong gamey taste. "If you're hungry enough, anything tastes good."

He shot her a quick glance as he pulled into the drive-through lane. "Sounds as if you're speaking from experience."

She nodded, regretting letting that statement slip out.

No reason for Rock to know how she and Darby had survived for weeks in the wilderness. As difficult as it had been to live off the land without so much as a tent for protection, she and Darby had reveled in the freedom.

And had silently vowed to never go back into the system, no matter what.

Rock gave the order for a full bucket of fried chicken along with mashed potatoes and green beans. She pulled out a twenty-dollar bill, but he waved her off.

"My treat," he said.

"You bought lunch," she pointed out.

"For Nora too," he countered. "And as a bribe to get you to report the tire slashing to Morrison. Fat lot of good that did," he added sourly.

She shook her head. "I told you it would be a waste of time and energy."

"It shouldn't have been." Rock's scowl deepened. "The guy is a disgrace to cops everywhere. The best we can hope for is that the incidents are on record. I highly doubt he followed through with any evidence collection."

Since her experience with cops was limited, and mostly bad, she didn't respond. Logically, she knew there had to be good cops out there, but she hadn't met very many.

Except for Rock. Who was a park ranger rather than a police officer. Granted, he had a badge and carried a gun, but his job was to protect the forest and the wildlife. A role she held in great esteem.

Animals deserved to be taken care of, allowed to roam free on the land. People needed to leave them alone.

She sighed and rubbed her temple. It would be nice if the shooter would leave her alone too.

The enticing scent of fried chicken filled the interior of the SUV, making her mouth water. She barely noticed when Rock pulled into the parking lot of a worn-down motel lit with a neon vacancy sign. The bucket of chicken was warm on her lap, and she was thinking of sneaking a bite to ward off her hunger pangs.

She told herself to get a grip. She wasn't a starving kid anymore. She could wait to eat until they were settled in the motel.

"I'll see if they have connecting rooms." Rock slid out from behind the wheel without looking at her. He shut the car door and strode inside.

His offer to pay for connecting rooms only made her feel worse about her earlier comment about spending the night with him. Why had she made such a ridiculous accusation?

*Because you like him. A lot.*

The realization struck deep. She drew in a deep breath and pulled her ragged emotions together. It didn't matter how much she liked or cared about Rock.

Life as she knew it here in Gatlinburg was over.

Time to start fresh, recreating herself in a new place where Darby, or whoever wanted her dead, would never find her.

ROCK WAS glad to find there were two connecting rooms available. Hailey's accusation stung, and he wanted to be sure she had the privacy she needed.

His admiration for her was at odds with his annoyance over her stubborn loner mentality. Would it kill her to accept a helping hand? To work with him on trying to figure out who was behind these attacks on her?

Taking the two room keys, he returned to the SUV. He

was grateful his vehicle hadn't been damaged by the gunfire. Even more glad Hailey had emerged from the incident unscathed.

He stood for a moment and looked up at the cloudless sky. God had certainly been watching over Hailey over the past twenty-four hours, and he silently thanked the Lord for doing so. It seemed clear that God had sent Rock to protect Hailey, and he was more than willing to step up to the challenge and do his part.

Which meant he needed to work extra hard at gaining Hailey's trust. Unfortunately, he was running out of time. He could understand Hailey's determination to keep Nora Rhodes and the kids and other visitors to the hobby farm safe. Something he should have considered when Nora begged him to stay, feeling certain Hailey was about to leave.

Nora's instincts had been right on target. And he was secretly pleased that Hailey hadn't taken the easy way out by stealing Nora's truck.

He slid behind the wheel. The fried chicken smelled delicious. "Here's your key, room seven. I'm in eight. I would respectfully ask that you unlock your side of the connecting rooms in case something bad happens."

"Okay." Her simple acquiescence surprised him.

"Thanks." He drove through the small parking lot and pulled up in front of his room. Before he could get out from behind the wheel, she handed him the bucket of chicken and hopped out of the car. She grabbed her backpack before he could offer to carry it for her.

"Smells good, doesn't it?" He offered a wry grin.

"Very much," she agreed with a smile. "I'll join you in a few minutes."

He nodded, watching for a moment as she unlocked her

motel room and stepped inside. He did the same, grimacing a bit at the tattered and worn interior of the room. He shouldn't have been surprised, he'd purposefully chosen the place because it was off the main road going through town and more likely to have available rooms in spite of the summer tourist season.

As he set the bucket of chicken on the small table, he heard the click as Hailey unlocked her side of the connecting door. He crossed over to open his side.

"Hope the room isn't too bad," he said, feeling self-conscious.

She lifted a brow. "Better than sleeping in the trolley station, or in the woods. I have a tent but had to repair the rips with duct tape. Difficult to know how well that'll hold up in the rain."

He shook his head, knowing she was right. He'd never in his life met a more self-sufficient woman, and that included the female rangers he'd worked with. "Let's eat."

Hailey didn't hesitate to join him at the table. He preferred to keep his faith private but decided that maybe he should include Hailey.

Clasping his hands, he bowed his head. "Dear Lord, we thank You for saving Hailey from being injured over these past twenty-four hours, and we ask that You continue to watch over and protect us as we attempt to find those responsible. Also, bless this food we are about to eat. Amen."

He looked up to find Hailey sitting with her arms crossed over her chest, a scowl on her features.

"What's wrong?" he asked, truly perplexed. Even those who didn't believe usually just sat silently while others prayed.

"God doesn't exist," she said in a flat tone.

Her stark statement caught him off guard. "I'm sorry you feel that way, although everyone is entitled to their own opinion. I truly believe the way you escaped serious injury over the past twenty-four hours is due to God's grace."

"Yeah? Where was He when we were being tortured by a man who liked to preach the word of God?" Hailey's outburst carried a level of venom he hadn't seen before. "There isn't a God, but there is a devil. I should know, I lived with him."

Hailey stood and disappeared through the connecting door. He winced when she slammed the door shut and threw the dead bolt home.

Wow. Okay, that didn't go well. He stared at the chicken, feeling sick to his stomach in the aftermath of her anger.

His intent had been to offer solace, but instead, he'd poked a festering wound. She'd been tortured by a man who preached the word of God? It was difficult to wrap his head around her accusation.

Yet it also explained a lot about Hailey's personality. As much as he felt bad for ruining the camaraderie between them, he knew that it was good for her to get some of that anger out of her system.

Bottled up anger could manifest itself in all sorts of ways. Drug and alcohol addiction, among others. He had to give Hailey credit that she hadn't ended up down that path.

Or had she?

The juvie record must be related in some way to the torture she'd experienced.

He bowed his head again, silently asking for the strength and wisdom he'd need to help Hailey through this.

After forcing himself to eat something, he crossed over to press his ear to the connecting door. There was nothing but silence on the other side. From what he could tell, Hailey didn't even have the television on.

Then again, he couldn't remember a television in her trailer, so maybe that form of entertainment didn't interest her.

Raking his hands through his hair, he tried to think of a way to convince her to eat something. The idea of her going hungry bothered him.

But he was hesitant to intrude on her solitude. Finally, he turned and grabbed the bucket of chicken. He set it right next to the connecting door, just in case she grew hungry later on in the night.

If she bothered to stay the night.

The keys to his SUV were in his pocket, but not having a ride wasn't much of a deterrent for her. Hailey had been prepared to walk all the way to the trolley station or sleep in the woods if needed.

In a damaged tent patched with duct tape.

He dropped onto the edge of the bed and cradled his head in his hands. He was emotionally and physically worn out. He hated knowing he'd inadvertently hurt Hailey and felt helpless about how to fix it.

Fixing things was what he did best. Hadn't his last girlfriend told him that? Courtney had claimed he cared more about fixing people than accepting them for who they were.

And she might have been right.

He wanted to fix this mess for Hailey in a big way.

As the sun disappeared behind the horizon, Rock stretched out on the bed fully dressed, listening for any sound coming from Hailey's room. He didn't want her to leave without his having the opportunity to change her mind.

Although she was free to leave if she chose to. His heart

felt heavy in the center of his chest, but he did his best to ignore the sensation.

Rock must have fallen asleep at some point, his exhaustion getting the better of him, because a soft click woke him up. Moving silently, he swung around to sit on the edge of the bed, trying to see through the dark interior of the room.

Had Hailey left the motel? He was about to head over to the window to see when he saw movement out of the corner of his eye.

The connecting door was open, and he could see Hailey's dark form standing there, hesitantly. For a long moment he didn't move, not even to breathe, afraid to do anything that might startle her and send her back to her room.

It was much the way he treated an injured wild animal, and that likeness to Hailey wasn't lost on him.

She bent down and picked up the bucket of chicken. The chicken, beans, and potatoes were likely cold, but he doubted she cared. She retreated into her room, but to his surprise, she didn't close and lock the connecting door.

A hint of trust? Maybe. He smiled like an idiot in the darkness and tiptoed back to the bed.

He fell asleep again, waking up to sunlight filtering through the darkness. He shot off the bed and rushed over to the connecting door.

It hung open about three inches. He pushed it farther and poked his head in.

His heart plummeted to the soles of his feet when he realized Hailey was gone.

## CHAPTER EIGHT

Hailey had awoken early, just as dawn crept over the horizon. She felt rested and, thanks to the chicken, potatoes, and green beans she'd eaten the night before, relatively satiated. There were leftovers, so she set them near the connecting door for Rock. It was only fair, considering he'd paid for the meal.

His prayer had brought a rush of horrible memories to the surface. Granted, he hadn't sounded anything like the Preacher, but the fact that Rock truly believed in a kind and loving God surprised her and sent her running away.

Embarrassed now to think about how she'd overreacted. She knew people believed in God, went to church, and prayed. She'd stayed in enough homeless shelters in those early days where you had to listen to a pastor before you'd get a meal.

But it had been easy to ignore those instances of preaching, compared to hearing Rock asking for strength and courage. With an effort, she shook off the impact of his words, even though she knew she wouldn't forget them. Hailey made use of the shower, especially since she had no idea when she'd have another opportunity to soak under a hot spray. Having clean hair and clean clothes felt wonderful, and she truly hated the idea of going back to washing up in gas station bathrooms.

Washing in the creek was a slightly better option. But that would have to wait until she reached her ultimate destination.

Wherever that was.

She grimaced. Running was what she did best. Being able to stay in one place for five years had been a gift. But also an illusion. She'd never been in one spot for this long before and look what had happened. Gunshots and vandalism.

Darby? Or someone else? Did it matter? Better to move on. Hopefully, it wouldn't take long for her to find a new job. And a place to live.

She took the small pencil and paper the motel provided and sat down, trying to think of a way to tell Rock goodbye.

Words didn't come easily. The Preacher's wife, Ruth, had homeschooled the foster kids as much as she could when the Preacher wasn't forcing them to kneel and repent. It wasn't that Hailey didn't know how to read and write, she did.

But putting her feelings on paper was incredibly difficult. In the end, she simply wrote: *Thank you for everything, Hailey.* It wasn't enough, but it would have to suffice. She set the note on top of the leftover chicken, then straightened. Determined to do what was necessary, she picked up her backpack and slid out the motel room door.

She crossed the parking lot, then paused and glanced back at the motel lobby. Through the window, she could see a small computer station. Available for guests to use? Must be, otherwise the owners would tuck it away in a back room somewhere.

Changing directions, she headed to the lobby. If she remembered correctly, the trolley station didn't open early. It was the one location in Gatlinburg where you could find a taxi that would take you to Knoxville for a flat, if pricy fee. And maybe she could spend a few minutes searching for Darby. It was an exercise she'd done several times before without success.

For all she knew, her foster sister might have changed her name. Hailey had entered the foster system knowing her last name was Donovan, but some of the other fosters, especially the young ones, didn't have the same privilege. Getting an ID and driver's license under her name hadn't been easy, until she found someone who'd agreed to forge a birth certificate and social security card.

Thankfully, Officer Morrison hadn't figured out the truth about her credentials. Rock either, for that matter.

Hailey entered the building, glancing around cautiously. There was an older woman behind the counter doing something on a computer screen. She ignored Hailey, which was fine with her.

Pretending as if she knew exactly what she was doing, Hailey strolled over, sat down, and clicked on the internet icon. She didn't have a lot of experience with computers, in fact, she'd never formally graduated high school, although she had earned her GED. Most of what she'd learned after escaping the Preacher had been centered around survival.

Looking at the trolley website first, she saw it opened at nine in the morning. Three hours from now, considering it was barely six. Once she took the taxi to Knoxville, she could hop a bus and head toward Nashville or in the opposite direction toward Asheville, North

Carolina. As much as she'd like to see the ocean, she knew that the bus would likely go through Cherokee to get to Asheville, and she couldn't force herself to go back there.

The Preacher's cabin had been in the hills outside of Cherokee. She'd arrived at the Preacher's cabin when she was nine years old and had escaped at fourteen.

Five long, painful years. Ironically as long as she'd been in Gatlinburg.

As always, thinking of the Preacher made her wonder where the rest of the fosters ended up. Jayme and Caitlin had gone north, while the boys had seemed to disappear in a southern direction.

She'd taken Darby west, ending up in Gatlinburg, then on to Pigeon Forge. After she'd gotten out of juvie, Hailey had searched for Darby, hoping and praying they could make amends, but when she didn't find her foster sister, she had taken the trolley back toward Gatlinburg, preferring it to Pigeon Forge.

Living here for the past five years had been the longest she'd spent anywhere other than the Preacher's cabin. The mountain tourist town had begun to feel like home.

The home she'd never had.

But not anymore. Her quick social media search for Darby brought up several possibilities. She peered closely at the screen, trying to recognize the photos as possibly belonging to her younger sister. But none of them looked even remotely familiar.

Hailey wasn't on social media either, so why would Darby be there? All this time she'd hoped her younger sister had done okay, but she knew there was a distinct possibility Darby hadn't.

It was an overwhelmingly depressing and discouraging

thought. If things had been different . . . maybe she could have steered Darby back on the right path.

And if wishes were coins, she'd be rich.

She decided to try Sawyer's name, including his last name, which he'd shared with her, staring in confusion when a photograph of a young man dressed in a police uniform bloomed on the screen.

Wait a minute. Sawyer was a cop? She stared incredulously at his picture. Officer Sawyer Murphy, age twenty-seven. He sure looked like her foster brother. She sat back in the chair with a reluctant smile.

Wow. How incredibly amazing that he'd been able to get his life together enough to become a cop. She'd barely managed to scrape out a living at the hobby farm in a low-budget rental trailer. She stared at the image in awe, proud of his success. Proof that escaping the Preacher had been the right thing to do.

Despite the troubles along the way.

Maybe Sawyer had received help to get where he was, and if so, more power to him. He'd been a good kid, always trying to protect the younger ones.

Her gaze widened when she realized he was a cop in Chattanooga, a city located in the most southern and eastern tip of Tennessee.

The urge to head that way to see him was strong. Sawyer knew about the Preacher, and maybe he even knew where the rest of the foster siblings were currently located. She glanced at the picture, noting it had been taken six years ago.

Was Sawyer still in Chattanooga? There was no way to know for sure.

She sat at the computer for so long, she didn't hear Rock

coming up behind her until she felt his hands on her shoulders. "I'm glad you're still here, Hailey."

His hands were warm, his musky scent teasing her senses. She quickly shut down the internet browser and pulled away to stand and face him.

"I'm heading over to the trolley station at nine, that's generally where the taxi cabs tend to hang out." She bent over to pick up her backpack. "You know it's best for Nora and the kids if I get out of town."

Rock held her gaze for a long moment. "I really wish you trusted me enough to help," he finally murmured. "You don't have to face the danger alone."

Alone. She swallowed hard at the lump of emotion that rose in the back of her throat. She'd been alone for so long, she didn't know how to be anything else. Nora was her closest friend and her boss, but even the woman she secretly looked up to like a mother didn't know the truth about her past.

Why was it so tempting to spill her guts to Rock?

"But if the station doesn't open until nine, we have time for breakfast," he continued. "There's a diner not far from here, we can walk over rather than drive if you'd prefer."

Spending more time with Rock was a bad idea. She was finding it difficult enough to leave Gatlinburg. As much as she liked the idea of heading to Chattanooga to possibly see Sawyer, it was difficult to know what her foster brother would think of her showing up after all this time.

Sawyer had obviously moved on with his life. Maybe he'd resent her dredging up the past.

And he might not still be in Chattanooga either.

"Please, Hailey, it can't be too much to ask to have breakfast together."

"Fine." She shouldered her pack. "But you're only

prolonging the eventual outcome, Rock." She followed him through the motel lobby. "I left you a note."

"I found it." He frowned. "Why on earth didn't you take the leftovers with you?"

"Because you paid for the meal."

"Hailey, it's killing me to know you're heading off on your own with nothing more than a roll of bills and a back-pack." He hunched his shoulders. "If you stayed in Gatlin-burg, we could work together to find out who is behind these attacks and arrest him. There's no need for you to start over someplace new."

She didn't answer. There was no point in rehashing the conversation. Rock assumed the shooter and knife-wielding vandal was a man, but she knew there was a chance the attacker was Darby.

Hailey kept coming back to the fact that Darby was the only person who'd been upset with her since they'd escaped the Preacher.

Rock pulled open the door of the diner, and she was immediately assailed by the twin aromas of coffee and bacon.

As if on cue, her stomach rumbled. She put a hand on her belly, hoping Rock hadn't heard.

"Let's grab a booth." Rock placed his hand in the small of her back and steered her toward it. If any other man had done that, she'd have snapped at him.

Somehow, she'd gotten so accustomed to being around Rock she barely noticed.

After sliding into the booth, she picked up the plastic menu and eyed the breakfast offerings. The prices were reasonable, and she made a silent vow to pay for her own food.

"My name is Maggie, would you like coffee?" A woman

roughly her own age came over carrying a pot of coffee and two mugs.

"Yes, please," she and Rock said at the same time.

Hailey laughed, a rusty sound even to her own ears. Rock's grin made her heart thump against her rib cage. She kept her gaze on Maggie pouring coffee, then drew her cup over and reached for the cream and sugar.

"That's a sound I'd like to hear more often," Rock said when Maggie moved away.

Her cheeks went pink. "Lately, there hasn't been much to laugh about."

"I know." Rock's intense hazel gaze made her feel like a bug pinned to a piece of cardboard. "All the more reason I'd love to hear more."

She averted her gaze, focusing on the menu. Soon, Maggie returned to take their order.

"I told my boss I couldn't come in to work today." Rock eyed her over the rim of his coffee mug. "First time I've taken a sick day in the past four years."

"Why?" She didn't want him taking off work for her. "I told you I'm leaving no matter what."

"Why not spend the day with me instead?" Rock countered. "We can ask around at the trailer park to see if anyone noticed someone hanging around, maybe even search for shell casings from the gunfire." He hesitated, then added, "If we don't find anything significant, I'll drive you to Knoxville so you don't have to pay for a taxi."

She wanted to stay, very much. Which only made her more determined not to.

"I don't think so, but thanks for the offer." He opened his mouth, but she held up a hand. "You know it's not likely anyone at the trailer park saw anything, or that they would tell us if they did. Let's just enjoy our meal, okay?"

Rock grimaced and looked away. Hailey tamped down a flash of guilt. She hadn't asked for him to call off work. She left a thank-you note, hadn't she? His wanting to help was sweet, but there wasn't much he could do.

Even if they found a suspicious person, or a shell casing, she highly doubted Morrison would go out of his way to investigate further.

One day of investigating wouldn't be enough. Leaving Gatlinburg was best done in a swift motion, like pulling a Band-Aid off your skin.

Painful at first, but the sensation would eventually fade.

And Hailey sensed if she didn't leave Gatlinburg soon, she wouldn't leave at all.

ROCK ATE HIS BREAKFAST, trying to think of a way to change Hailey's mind. He'd used every argument he could come up with, but she was more stubborn than Rory the kicking donkey or Lucy the spitting llama.

By the time they'd finished eating, he was no closer to convincing her to stay. When she pulled out her cash to pay, he tried waving her off, but she wasn't having it.

"I'd prefer to pay my own way," she said. Then added, "Please."

"Okay," he said in a resigned tone. At least breakfast wasn't expensive, but he wished she'd save what money she had to get through the next few days.

"I'll drive you to Knoxville," he offered as a last-ditch effort to help her out. "No reason to waste your cash on a taxi."

"No thanks." They left the diner, and she turned to face

him. "Rock, I really do appreciate everything you've done for me. But you have to let me go. It's safer for everyone."

"Okay." What could he do? Short of hog-tying her and tossing her into the back of his SUV, she was free to leave.

"Go to work," she added, shouldering her pack. "I don't want you to risk your job for me."

"I don't think one day off will get me fired," he said mildly. "I'd sleep better knowing you're safe."

She rolled her eyes and turned away. "Bye, Rock." She strode purposefully toward the street leading to the trolley station.

Turning away from Hailey was the hardest thing he'd ever done. And it didn't even make any sense for him to feel her leaving so keenly. They barely knew each other, yet his emotions were all tangled in knots over her.

His plan to investigate the attacks against her had been a long shot anyway. He investigated poachers and other crimes that took place on state parkland, and he knew this was a job for the local police.

Since he was in town, he abruptly decided to show up at police headquarters. It would make him feel better to make sure others knew about Morrison's lousy investigation of the three separate incidents. And he may as well add the most recent information regarding the attempt on the highway to the list of attacks.

He returned to the motel to pick up his SUV. He drove to the police station and strode purposefully inside.

"May I help you?" A female officer was seated at the front desk.

"I'm Park Ranger Rock Wilson," he said, offering his badge. "I'd like to speak to the day shift sergeant please." Rock was familiar with law enforcement hierarchy and hoped Morrison's boss would prove to be a better and more honorable cop.

"Just a moment." She picked up the phone and pushed a button. "Sergeant Kellen? I have a Park Ranger Wilson who would like to see you." After a moment, she nodded. "Yes, sir." She hung up the phone and gestured toward the door leading to the back where he could see several cubicles and desks. "Sergeant Kellen is straight down the hall and to the right. But you have to leave your weapon with me." She gestured toward the lockbox beside her.

Standard protocol, so he didn't argue and set the gun in the lockbox. "Thanks." Rock easily found Kellen, who appeared to be a decade younger than Morrison. "Sergeant Kellen, I appreciate you seeing me."

"Of course, what can I do for you?" Kellen gestured to the chair across from his desk.

"I have a complaint about Officer Morrison."

A flicker of anger flashed in Kellen's eyes, and Rock knew he wasn't the first to complain about the guy. Kellen straightened. "What seems to be the problem?"

Rock explained about the multiple assaults toward Hailey. "Morrison never bothered to interview the other residents in the trailer park or have a crime scene tech check the trailer for fingerprints," Rock said tersely. "If there were any clues to be found, they're likely useless by now."

Kellen grimaced and nodded. "I'll take care of that, thanks for letting me know. Although I find it interesting you've shown up here without the victim."

"The victim is scared to death and wants to leave town because she knows Morrison hasn't taken her attacks seriously," Rock snapped. He rose to his feet. "Morrison's investigation skills are a disgrace, he shouldn't be allowed to carry a badge. If anything happens to Hailey Donovan, the blame rests solely with you and this lame excuse for a police department." He stalked off, fighting to keep his temper under control. Grabbing his gun from the lockbox, he headed outside.

He should have felt better after unloading on Sergeant Kellen, but he didn't. It was too little, too late. He should have made the trip yesterday, not that it would have prevented Hailey from leaving.

She'd made that decision earlier in the day.

Rock stepped outside and glanced up at the sky. Dark clouds were rolling in from the west, and he could taste the hint of rain in the air.

Did Hailey have a raincoat or an umbrella? He told himself she'd be fine, especially since she'd be in a taxi.

He had to stop worrying about her.

Even if he couldn't seem to pry her from his mind.

He'd never called off work for a woman before. He climbed into his SUV and drove out of the police station parking lot, toward the highway that would take him home.

He could call his boss, tell him he was feeling better and would report to work within the hour. Glancing at the dashboard clock, he wondered if Hailey had found a taxi yet. There was no bus station in town, so anyone visiting Gatlinburg generally drove a car or took a taxi into town from Knoxville. But he figured those using taxi cabs were few and far between.

For some inexplicable reason, he found himself turning and heading to the bus station. He knew she wouldn't change her mind about leaving, but if a taxi didn't show up soon, maybe she'd take him up on his offer to driver her. At the very least, she might appreciate knowing he'd reported Morrison for being a lousy cop.

And wasn't that the lamest excuse on the planet?

He parked and went inside the lobby area of the transit station. The place was more crowded than he'd expected, thanks to the summer tourists milling about.

Raking his gaze over the lobby area, he found Hailey sitting off in the corner by herself. She looked miserable, as if she might be close to crying.

He hadn't realized until that moment how much she really didn't want to leave Gatlinburg. That she really was doing the honorable thing by leaving to keep Nora and the kids safe.

Before he could head over to her, she swiped at her face, stood, and grabbed her backpack.

She headed toward the restrooms located in the far corner of the room. He thought he'd wait for her, but then he noticed a man wearing a baseball hat pulled low over his eyes following her.

With a frown, Rock moved forward in time to see the man stealthily reach into his pocket and pull out a knife.

"Hailey, knife!" he shouted, breaking into a run. "Stop him, he has a knife!"

Hailey whirled toward the assailant as people screamed and scattered in several directions.

Rock pushed his way toward Hailey, hoping and praying he wasn't too late.

## CHAPTER NINE

Hailey reacted instinctively to Rock's shout and swung her backpack directly at the man looming behind her. She hit his outstretched hand with enough force that the knife clattered to the floor.

The assailant whirled and ran, dodging people who were also trying to get away from the scene. Rock stumbled over a small suitcase but didn't go down. Hailey stood frozen in place, hardly able to believe it when Rock appeared at her side. His concerned gaze raked over her.

"Are you hurt? Did he cut you?" Rock grasped her arm, then surprised her by pulling her into his arms. She surprised herself by letting him. Their embrace only lasted a moment, before he noticed the knife on the floor. He pulled away and stepped on the knife to keep it from being disturbed.

"What are you doing here?" Her mind seemed to have short-circuited by both the attack and Rock's warm embrace. "I thought you'd be back up in the mountains by now."

"I was too busy filing a complaint about Morrison with

his boss." Rock turned and swept a glance over the lobby. "Did you get a good look at the guy? I should have chased him down, but I was worried he'd cut you."

"I didn't recognize him." Hailey pulled herself together with an effort. Seeing the man behind her, a stranger with a knife, had knocked her off balance.

Not Darby, or any of her foster brothers. Not even Darby's old boyfriend, Aaron.

A stranger.

Why had a stranger tried to stab her with a knife?

"I'm calling Sergeant Kellen," Rock said grimly. "The knife is evidence, and I want it dusted for prints."

*A stranger.* She still couldn't come to grips with the fact that a complete stranger had tried to hurt her.

Then she realized the guy could be Darby's boyfriend. Not Aaron, she'd have recognized him, but maybe another man her sister was involved with? The guy who'd attacked her was probably in his late thirties, early forties, a lot older than her foster sister, but that didn't mean much. Although if he was Darby's boyfriend, where was she? If Darby was holding a grudge to the point of wanting to harm Hailey, surely she'd be close by.

Or was it possible none of this was connected to her time with the Preacher?

"Hailey? Did you hear me?"

Rock's words belatedly penetrated the fog in her brain. "Yeah. Who's Sergeant Kellen?"

"Morrison's boss." Rock held his phone up to his ear. "This is Park Ranger Rock Wilson again. I need Sergeant Kellen to report to the transit station ASAP. There's been another attempt on Hailey Donovan's life. Do not send Officer Morrison in his place, understand? Good." He lowered his phone and blew out a breath. "Kellen will be here shortly."

"I can't believe you went over Morrison's head," she murmured. "He's not going to be happy about that."

"Like I care? Look what almost happened here in a public place?" Rock's frustration wasn't aimed at her, but she took a step back anyway. "That man tried to stab you."

"I know." She was shaken by the near miss. "I can't believe he did that in the middle of the trolley station."

"Hailey, please don't leave." His hazel gaze pleaded with her. "For one thing, he might know where you're headed. The taxis only go as far as Knoxville and back. And secondly, there's a good chance we'll get some evidence off the knife. If we find the identity of this guy, we can lock him up, and you can safely go back home."

A flare of hope bloomed in her chest at the possibility of not needing to leave Gatlinburg and the hobby farm. She glanced down at the knife beneath his hiking boot. "You might be right about the evidence. I don't remember him wearing gloves."

"And he didn't look familiar?" Rock pressed.

She met his gaze dead-on. "Not one bit. I swear, Rock, I've never seen that man before in my life."

He stared into her eyes for a long moment before nodding. "I believe you. I know you haven't told me everything, but I believe you didn't recognize him."

There was no way to argue his instincts, and she had to squelch the urge to tell him about her foster siblings. Instead, she focused on what she remembered.

"He was about five-nine or five-ten, on the heavier side, with a full beard, and light brown hair that looked unkempt beneath the baseball cap." She frowned, then added, "If I had to guess his age, I'd say late thirties or early forties."

"Good description," Rock praised. "Maybe you could work with a sketch artist."

She hesitated. "I don't know, Rock. I guess I could stay for a while." Then she frowned. "Wait a minute, how did the knife guy even know I was here?"

Rock's expression turned grim. "He might have gotten a glimpse of my license plate number and followed us."

"You didn't drive me here, I walked, remember?" Had the knife guy followed her from the café? If so, she hadn't noticed, which meant she was really slipping.

And why? That was the part that didn't make any sense.

"Here's Sergeant Kellen," Rock said, lifting his hand and waving the cop over. "Hopefully, he's a better investigator than Morrison."

Anyone was better than Morrison, but she didn't voice her thought. Sergeant Kellen was younger than Morrison, his expression intense as he came toward them. She wondered how Morrison felt reporting to a guy at least ten years his junior.

"Ranger Wilson?" Kellen raked his gaze over them. "This must be Hailey Donovan."

"Yes." She lifted her chin, wondering if the sergeant had already performed a background check on her. "This is the second, no third attempt to hurt me, and I've also been the victim of two episodes of vandalism."

"I witnessed a man wearing a dark blue T-shirt, black jeans, and a navy blue baseball cap low over his eyes follow Ms. Donovan toward the restrooms," Rock said. "When he pulled the knife from his pocket, I shouted at Hailey. She turned and used her backpack to knock the knife from his hand. He took off running, but the knife is here." Rock gestured to the floor where the knife lay. "I don't remember him wearing gloves, so we should be able to lift a few prints off it."

Kellen nodded slowly. He pulled an evidence bag from his pocket and bent down to pick up the knife. "Okay, what about a description of the guy?"

Hailey repeated what she remembered of what he looked like. Sergeant Kellen took some notes, then glanced around the trolley station lobby. "I'll have a few officers interview these people to see if they have anything to add."

"Not Morrison," Rock said firmly.

Kellen reluctantly nodded. "Not Morrison. Yours was the second complaint I've gotten about him, and the most credible. As such, I've put him on desk duty for the foreseeable future."

"Good and thanks." Rock held out his hand to Sergeant Kellen. "I'm sorry to create issues for you, but I know Morrison didn't take these attacks against Ms. Donovan seriously."

"I hate to admit I agree with you." Kellen held up the bag containing the knife. "It's a typical hunting knife, nothing unusual, but we'll get this tested for fingerprints right away." Sergeant Kellen turned toward her. "Ms. Donovan, I would really like you to come to the station to write up a formal statement. And to work with a sketch artist to see if we can get a likeness on this guy."

Rock had warned her about the sketch artist, and since this was the closest they'd come to actually figuring out who was behind these attacks, she nodded. "Okay."

She heard Rock expel a pent-up breath of relief.

Sergeant Kellen spoke into his radio, and soon they were joined by two officers. One was older than Morrison, the other younger than the sergeant. Kellen quickly read off her brief description and told the officers to question all the people in the bus depot.

"You better hurry," Hailey said. "The ten o'clock bus to Knoxville is leaving soon, and some of these people will likely be on it."

Leaving the officers to their job, she and Rock followed the sergeant outside. "Meet you at the police station," Kellen said.

"Will do." Rock gestured toward his SUV. "We'll drive over, if that's okay."

"Sure." There was no reason to argue as there was no sign of a taxi anyway. "I hope they find something on that knife."

"Me too." Rock glanced at her. "Thanks for staying, Hailey."

"For now," she agreed. The ride to the police station didn't take long. As she followed Rock inside, waiting as he locked up his weapon at the front desk, she wondered if they'd really identify the man who'd tried to stab her.

And if the guy turned out to be Darby's boyfriend? She grimaced and silently acknowledged that she'd find a way to deal with that later.

Protecting Darby was one thing, but that didn't mean she was interested in protecting her sister's boyfriend, if that's who this guy was.

If she was the type to pray, she'd ask God to make sure Darby wasn't involved in this.

That none of the fosters were involved.

Too bad God had stopped listening to her prayers long ago.

ROCK TRIED NOT to let his jubilation show, even though he was crazy relieved Hailey was staying.

Turned out to be a good thing he'd called off work. Maybe later, once they had an identity of the guy who'd tried to shoot Hailey, he could explain everything to his boss. Technically, he was working, investigating the gunfire on national parkland, although his boss may not see it that way.

He didn't care, even if he did get stuck with the lousy shifts because of it. He was glad to know God was watching over Hailey, whether she believed it or not.

"Have a seat in here." Kellen waved toward the door of a small interview room.

"Thanks," Hailey said. Rock followed her into the room, taking a seat next to her.

The way she twisted her fingers together indicated she was nervous. "There's nothing to worry about," he reassured her. "This is routine stuff."

"Easy for you to say," she murmured. "You haven't been on the wrong side of the police, have you?"

"No," he admitted. She'd never mentioned what had happened that she'd ended up serving time as a juvenile. "But you're the victim here, Hailey."

She shrugged, not looking convinced. Kellen returned with a pad of paper and a pen. The sergeant took a seat across from them.

"Why don't you start at the very beginning?" he suggested, pushing the tablet of paper toward her.

Hailey hesitated for a long moment, before drawing the paper and pen toward her. For a horrible moment, Rock feared she might not know how to read and write.

"Okay, I'll start with the shooting on the hiking trail." He relaxed when Hailey took the pen and began writing.

She seemed to be making an effort to print clearly, and his heart squeezed in his chest at how unfamiliar writing seemed to be for her.

What in the world had her life been like before she'd ended up in Gatlinburg? He wanted to pull her into his arms and convince her that he'd always be there to protect her.

Even though that was physically impossible. Even if she did stay in Gatlinburg, he couldn't be glued to her side twenty-four seven.

Could he?

He gave himself a mental shake. No, he couldn't. Besides, there was no reason to be fascinated by a woman who'd had a rough life. Lots of people overcame insurmountable odds to become contributing members of society. Hailey was one of many.

Yet he sensed that her intense reaction to his prayer was somehow related to whatever had caused her to end up in juvie.

Maybe someday she'd trust him enough to tell her story.

Kellen disappeared, saying something about getting the sketch artist in. Rock sat back, waiting patiently as Hailey painstakingly wrote out her story.

After a good fifteen minutes, she put the pen down and pushed the pad of paper away. "Glad that's over," she muttered.

"It's important to have it documented in your own words," he pointed out. "And the sketch artist will be here soon."

"How long to get the fingerprints back?"

He shrugged. "It doesn't take long to lift the prints from an object like a knife. The problem will be in searching AFIS for a potential match." He hesitated, then added, "If this guy doesn't have a criminal record, or wasn't in a role where prints were taken, this could be a dead end."

"Great." She sighed. "Just what we need, another dead end."

"Let's try to think positive, okay?" He offered a weary smile. "You've been able to avoid being hurt so far, right?"

She turned in her seat to face him. "Yes, but why were you at the trolley station?"

He didn't want to put her off by talking about God, although he firmly believed God had sent him there to protect her. "I'm not sure how to answer you," he said finally. "Deep down, I guess I wanted to see you one last time."

Her blue eyes widened. "Rock, you're going to have to let me go sooner or later."

It was on the tip of his tongue to ask why when the door to the interview room opened revealing Sergeant Kellen. "Sketch artist is here. I'll send her in."

"I'm ready," Hailey said.

A young woman came into the room, holding a large sketchpad and a tray of chalk. "Hi, I'm Amber."

"Hailey. It's nice to meet you. Although, I hope you're not expecting too much of me, I've never worked with a sketch artist before."

"Most victims haven't," Amber assured her. "No worries. It's my job to pull as much detail from you as possible. And from what I hear, you've been a great witness so far."

Rock stood, offering the chair next to Hailey. "I'll be back in a few minutes, okay?"

"Sure," Hailey agreed.

He left the women alone and went to search for Sergeant Kellen. When he came upon a desk where

Morrison sat with a phone up to his ear, he slowed and made a point of looking at the cop directly in the eye.

Morrison sneered, then looked away. Rock shouldn't have gotten a surge of satisfaction from the wordless exchange, but he did.

Maybe the next time Morrison responded to a call he'd act like the professional his uniform demanded him to be. Every victim, no matter what their background, should be treated with dignity and respect.

He paused outside Sergeant Kellen's office, listening as the guy finished up a call. When he hung up, Rock stepped in. "I don't suppose you have anything on the fingerprints yet?"

"No. But that was one of my officers at the transit station. There is a general consensus as to the perp's description as provided by Ms. Donovan. Unfortunately, we don't have a clear view of him from any of the cameras either. His hat covers his face."

"Figures," Rock said. "No additional information?"

"No identifying marks or clothing labels," Kellen confirmed. "Hey, I'm impressed we had people who described the same guy. Eyewitnesses are notoriously unreliable."

"True." Rock's experience was similar. "The sketch might help."

Kellen nodded, then sat back in his seat, eyeing him thoughtfully. "What's your interest in this case, Wilson?"

He frowned. "The gunfire aimed at Ms. Donovan came within inches of striking me too. Call me crazy, but I don't like it when people recklessly shoot at other people."

"Yeah, I get that," Kellen conceded. "But I sense you have a very personal stake in the outcome of this case."

Rock did, but he wasn't ready to admit it. At least, not to

Kellen. His feelings toward Hailey were—complicated. Holding her in his arms had felt right, and he'd been surprised she hadn't punched him as a result. "It also bothers me when cops who should uphold the law don't do their jobs," he added. "Trust me, if Morrison had taken the threat against Ms. Donovan seriously, I wouldn't have escalated my concerns to you."

"Yeah, okay." Kellen's penetrating gaze indicated he didn't entirely believe it. But before he could say anything, his phone rang. "Kellen," he answered curtly.

Rock moved away from the doorway in an effort to give the sergeant some privacy, but Kellen waved him in. The sergeant listened intently for a few moments, then said, "Okay, bag it and bring it in as evidence. Sounds like there's a good chance we'll get hair follicle DNA off it."

Rock's pulse quickened. "The hat? You found the guy's baseball hat?"

"My officers did, yes. At least we think so, no way to know for sure since it's dark blue and has no logo. It was found about twenty feet from the bus depot doorway."

"Getting DNA from it would be great." Rock was thrilled with the discovery.

"Again, there's no way to know for sure the hat belongs to the perp," Kellen said hastily. "But if we get prints, and this guy is in the system, any DNA we can get from the hat will clinch the arrest."

"Great work, Sergeant," Rock praised. "Thanks."

"We don't have anyone in custody yet," Kellen protested. "You know as well as I do that solid police work takes time."

"I know." Yet Rock couldn't deny the flash of anticipation. The guy had made a big mistake going after Hailey in a public place, and he was glad the police were able to capitalize on it. "Keep me posted about the fingerprints."

"Sure thing. Always happy to cooperate with the park rangers," Kellen agreed.

Rock turned and made his way back to the interview room. He was only involved in one other case where a sketch artist was used, and the process had been time-consuming.

He was pleasantly surprised to see that Amber had already made decent progress on the sketch, no doubt because Hailey had provided a detailed description.

They were still working on the eyes, and Rock was forced to admit that he wasn't as much help as Hailey. He hadn't focused his attention on the guy's face, his gaze riveted by the knife in his hand.

Everything had happened so fast, and he wished again he'd have taken off after the guy. If he'd caught him, they'd have him in jail, and Hailey would already be back to working on Nora's hobby farm.

And he'd have a chance to ask her out on a proper date.

Whoa, where had that thought sprung from? Hailey wasn't interested in dating him. Hadn't he sworn off women anyway? Especially those who didn't want to be fixed?

Not to mention, she wasn't a believer. He'd learned from painful experience that trying to change women's minds about faith and God was useless. Courtney certainly hadn't wanted to discuss the possibility. Which is why she'd claimed he refused to accept her the way she was, without trying to change her.

"How's this?" Amber said, breaking into his thoughts.

Hailey stared at the likeness for a long moment. "It's pretty close," she agreed. "Considering I only got a quick glimpse of him. I can't think of anything to add or change."

"You did amazingly well," Amber assured her. "I'll get this to the sergeant. I think he's planning to distribute the image to all his officers in an effort to find him."

"Looks great to me too," Rock agreed. The door to the interview room opened, and Kellen stood there, a grim expression on his face.

And just like that, the balloon of hope in his chest burst. "What is it?"

"No hit on the partial print we lifted from the knife," Kellen said. "Apparently, our perp doesn't have a criminal record."

It was the news he'd feared. He glanced at Hailey, who looked equally dejected.

He knew without her saying a word she still planned to leave town. Somehow, he needed to convince her to stay.

## CHAPTER TEN

Hailey knew she shouldn't have gotten her hopes up about the possibility of finding this guy. It was frustrating to have seen and caught him in action, only to have him slip away.

She looked again at the sketch Amber had completed. It wasn't as good as a photograph, but was it possible that the likeness would lead to an arrest?

"Don't worry, Hailey," Rock assured her. "We still have a good chance at finding this guy. The officers at the bus depot found a navy blue baseball hat about twenty yards from the doorway. They're checking to see if they can get DNA from any hair follicles or sweat from it."

"DNA would be great, but we need a suspect to match it, right?" Again, she wasn't about to get her hopes up. She could head back to the transit station to see if she could grab a taxi, but if not, she'd feel like a sitting duck. She could give in and ask Rock to take her, but she felt certain he'd continue to badger her about staying.

"Hailey?" Rock's intense gaze was impossible to ignore. "Give the police some time, okay? They have the sketch and could get this guy in custody very soon."

"I don't know what to do," she reluctantly admitted. "I know it's possible they'll find this guy, but I need to find a new job, ASAP." And a place to live, she added silently.

"Please let me help you," Rock said softly. "I know how much you enjoy your job at the hobby farm. If you'd just trust me for a little while longer, I'm sure we can get this guy."

"I trust you more than most," she said with a weary smile.

"I'm glad." His grin was dazzling. "Please, Hailey. Don't leave without giving us a chance." He seemed to realize what he'd said and hastily amended it to, "Without giving the police a chance to find this guy. I can protect you if you'll let me."

She knew Rock was capable of protecting her, but the real problem was that she liked him more than she should. That she longed to be held in his arms again.

Ridiculous longing, as Rock believed in God and she only believed in the devil.

A devil who'd pretended to be a preacher.

"Twenty-four hours," Rock pressed. "One more day. I promise to drive you to Knoxville myself, if you're still determined to go."

Suddenly she couldn't fight Rock and her own desire to stay in Gatlinburg any longer. "One day," she agreed.

"Great." Rock's relief was evident on his features. "Thanks, Hailey."

She nodded and edged toward the door. "Is it okay if we leave the police station now?"

"Of course." He stopped at the desk long enough to retrieve his weapon, then crossed the room, held the door open, and followed her outside.

The fresh air was wonderful, despite the heat of the

sun. She closed her eyes and lifted her face to the warmth, doing her best to let go of the past.

Being inside the police station had stirred old memories of her arrest, and the cop who'd tried to barter sex in exchange for letting her go. She shivered and shook off the memories. Having a juvie record was worth it. Especially when she'd told her lawyer about what the cop had done, he'd told her it was the cop's word against hers, and it wasn't likely she'd be believed. Yet she'd always thought the main reason she'd gotten off as lightly as she had was because the cop involved was asked about her allegation and ended up dropping the charge to a lesser offense.

"Would you like me to get the connecting rooms at the motel again?" Rock asked.

She nodded. "Staying in town close to the police station would probably be best."

"All right, we'll drive over in my SUV."

Remembering the possibility of the SUV being followed into town in the first place made her put a hand on Rock's arm. "Maybe we should walk instead. Keep your SUV here in the police parking lot. Less likely to be hit by vandalism while parked here, right?"

He stared at her for a long moment before nodding. "You make a good point."

The motel they'd stayed in wasn't far, although with the sun beating down on them, they were both hot and sweaty by the time they arrived. Hailey set her backpack down and waited outside as Rock went in to secure the rooms.

She swept her gaze over the area, looking for the knife guy. But all she saw were tourists and locals going about their business. A flash of guilt hit hard when she thought of Nora working the hobby farm alone.

Yet putting her or any of the kids in danger wasn't an option.

When Rock returned with two keys for their same rooms, she asked, "Is it okay to make local calls from the room?"

"Yes, why?"

"I feel like I should call Nora to explain why I left. I would have called her from my trailer, but my phone was busted up. And I completely forgot after being shot at on the highway."

"I have a phone. You can use mine or the one in your room to call Nora." He opened the door to his room, eyeing her speculatively. "You can call others, too, if you'd like."

So Rock had gotten a glimpse of her internet search earlier that morning. She thought about Sawyer and nodded. "I'd like that."

"I hope you're not getting in touch with your old boyfriend," Rock said with a frown. "He hasn't exactly been cleared as a suspect."

"Jacob? No." She picked up her backpack, then accessed her room. "Why would I do something like that?"

"I don't know, Hailey. You haven't really said anything about what your plans are other than getting out of town."

He was right. She wasn't used to being accountable to anyone about what she was doing. Jacob had always been annoyed when she'd decided to go hiking without telling him, as if she shouldn't dare make plans without him.

She entered her room, tossed her backpack onto the bed, and headed over to unlock the dead bolt on the connecting door. Their rooms had been cleaned in their absence, but the faint scent of fried chicken lingered in the air.

Wrinkling her nose, she realized she didn't want to be

sitting inside the motel room all day. When she returned to the connecting door, she noted Rock had opened his side as well.

"You mentioned I could borrow your phone?"

"Sure." Rock quickly handed it to her.

She stared at it for a moment, then resolutely punched in the number for the hobby farm. Nora didn't answer, no doubt her hands full of kids, so she left a quick message. "Nora, I'm sorry I didn't come in, but there was another attempt to shoot me, and I can't risk anything happening to you or the kids. Again, I'm sorry." She quickly disconnected and handed the phone back to Rock.

"You mentioned calling someone else too," he reminded her.

Sawyer. She hesitated, then shook her head. If she had the opportunity to talk to her foster brother, she didn't want Rock listening in. "No need."

He eyed her thoughtfully as he pocketed the phone, and she realized he knew she didn't want to make the call in front of him.

Rock could read her better than most, which was a bit disturbing. Especially since she worked hard to keep people at arm's length.

Except maybe for Nora.

"I think we should set up a plan to draw knife guy out," she abruptly declared.

Rock frowned. "What? No way."

"Why not?" She waved an impatient hand. "I don't want to sit inside all day, what else are we going to do? I guess we could walk around and try to find the guy ourselves, but it would be much better for me to sit out in the open to draw him out of hiding."

Rock's expression turned incredulous. "You want to set

yourself up as bait? And what if he uses a gun next time, instead of a knife?"

She truly hadn't considered that possibility but easily dismissed it. "He's not going to use a gun in the middle of town, too many people around."

"He might not make another attempt to hurt you at all, after being nearly caught in the bus depot," Rock pointed out.

If that was the case, there was no need for her to stick around. Yet she didn't really believe it. "He hasn't stopped so far, has he?" she countered. "Twice with a gun, two episodes of vandalism, and an attempt to stab me. Safe to assume he'll try again."

"I refuse to use you as bait, Hailey." Rock's tone was firm. "Let the police do their job."

"You can't stop me, Rock," she said softly. "And I can't just sit in the room doing nothing. That's not my style." She hesitated, then added, "I tend to be a bit claustrophobic."

He let out a heavy sigh. "We can hike one of the trails. I think the River View Trail is within walking distance of here."

It was a sweet offer and proved he knew her better than most. "Rock, as much as I enjoy hiking, that's not going to help us find this guy. Which is the whole reason I agreed to stay another twenty-four hours," she added.

"Hailey . . ." Rock sighed again.

"Come with me or not, your choice." She glanced at the clock on the nightstand. "It'll be lunchtime soon. Maybe we can sit outside at a café."

"Okay, I'll come with you." His closed expression indicated that he was not happy. "But I truly believe the police will pick him up very soon."

She didn't nearly have his level of faith. Not in the local cops or in a higher power.

They wandered down the main thoroughfare, hopefully giving the impression of being tourists, despite Rock still wearing his uniform.

When they found a corner café with outdoor seating beneath brightly colored umbrellas, Rock led her toward it. As she scanned the menu, she looked for something cheap but filling.

Neither of them said anything as they sat near the sidewalk, watching people stroll past. It occurred to Hailey that this idea of drawing the knife guy out of hiding might not be at all effective.

She'd learned patience at an early age, but it was still difficult to sit and wait for knife guy to strike.

And to be honest, she really hoped he'd try again. If he did, there was no way she'd let him get away.

---

HATING every minute of this insane plan, Rock sat tensely across from Hailey at the café. At first he tried to keep up a keen surveillance of the people walking past them, but it was impossible to see anything unusual with all the activity.

Which only proved that this idea was ludicrous. The knife-wielding guy could be upon Hailey before Rock realized what was happening.

The hiking idea had been a good compromise. Clearly, Hailey wasn't the type to sit around inside a motel room. Or any other enclosed space. Except maybe a tent. He sipped his iced tea as they waited for their lunch order. Maybe she'd get tired of being bait and agree to the hike after they finished eating.

He could tell she was already getting antsy.

The idea of her losing patience with this plan had him relaxing in his seat. His phone vibrated. With a grimace, he took his phone from his pocket and peered at the screen.

His boss, no doubt angry at his calling off work.

Pushing the button to ignore the call, he set the phone aside.

"I hope you're not in trouble with your boss," Hailey said.

He should have known she'd figure out who'd called. He shrugged. "Your safety is more important."

"Rock . . ." Her voice trailed off. "You shouldn't put your job at risk because of me."

Her statement irked him. Leaning forward, he pinned her with an intense gaze. "You don't know me very well if you think I value a job over someone's life."

Contrite, she looked away. "Thank you."

"You're welcome." He gestured to the phone. "If you want to make your call, feel free. I'm going to the restroom." He stood and deliberately walked away, hoping she'd take advantage of the opportunity to make her secret call while he was gone.

He used the facilities, then stared at his reflection in the mirror as he washed his hands. With a grimace, he silently admitted he was becoming emotionally attached to Hailey in a way that wasn't healthy.

Not least of all because she didn't feel the same way toward him. Grateful? Sure. Willing to spend time with him? Yep, that too.

But anything more? No way.

His problem, not hers.

When he'd dawdled long enough, he returned to the table, once again searching for anyone resembling the sketch

Amber created. His phone was right where he'd left it, and he sadly realized she hadn't taken advantage of the opportunity.

Before he could ask her about it, their server approached with their meals. He'd ordered a buffalo chicken wrap, while Hailey had gotten a turkey club.

He bowed his head and silently prayed for God's blessing over their food and over their safety. He knew God was watching over them and silently thanked Him for that too.

When he lifted his head, he was surprised to see that Hailey was sitting with her hands in her lap, staring down at her meal. Not likely praying but in an effort to respect his prayer.

"Thank you, Hailey," he murmured. "Looks good, doesn't it?" He lifted his buffalo chicken wrap and took a big bite.

"Very," she agreed, sampling her wrap. "Oh, and thanks for letting me borrow your phone."

He glanced at the device on the table. He picked it up and noticed she'd made a call. He frowned and looked at her. "The Chattanooga police station?"

She shrugged. "A friend of mine works there."

A male friend? The stab of jealousy was unwelcome. He did his best to ignore it. "I'm glad you were able to connect with your friend."

"He wasn't at his desk, so I left a message."

So, it was a man. Rock told himself to get over it. "I guess you're planning a visit, huh? I'm sure there's a bus from Knoxville to Chattanooga."

"Maybe," was her noncommittal response. "I haven't seen him in thirteen years, so I'm not sure he'll be thrilled if I show up unannounced."

Thirteen years? Not a boyfriend, then. And it explained her computer search. "Oh, I'm sure he'll be glad to reconnect with you."

She took another bite of her wrap, eyeing him curiously. "I'm sure you've figured out by now I didn't have an idyllic childhood."

Thrilled that she was talking about her past at all, he slowly nodded. "Yes, Hailey. But you've done an admiral job of overcoming whatever transpired back then."

She arched a brow. "Is that a compliment?"

He flushed. "Well yeah, that's how I meant it. Not everyone is able to put their tumultuous past behind them to move on the way you have."

Hailey shrugged and reached for her iced tea. "I'm not sure I've done a good job of putting it all behind me, but at least I'm doing something positive with my life." She frowned, and added, "Or I was. Until someone started using me for target practice."

The threat was more serious than that, but he didn't correct her. "Hailey, I admire you for what you've accomplished."

"Working at a hobby farm?" Her laugh sounded hollow. "Yeah, that's impressive all right."

"I watched you with those kids," he said as if she hadn't spoken. "They were interested in what you had to say, and they enjoyed interacting with the animals. Maybe it's not rocket science, but you're touching the lives of kids all across the area. That's very important, Hailey."

A faint smile tugged at her features. "I think that's probably the nicest thing anyone has said to me."

It was a sad testament. He wanted very much to reach across the table to take her hand, but he didn't dare. She'd tolerated their brief embrace, but likely out of fear and confusion more than anything.

His prickly porcupine now resembled a skittish wild mare. He didn't want to scare her off, yet he longed for something deeper.

"You deserve so much more," he murmured. "And I really wish you'd give me a chance."

"I am giving you a chance, Rock. I trust you, more than you realize." Her smile was lopsided. "I shouldn't even be sitting here with you. Not when logic tells me I should be getting far away from this guy, whoever he is."

Her admission warmed his heart. "I'm glad you agreed to stay, at least for a while." He thought for a minute, then added, "In fact, I think deep down you don't want to give up the life you've made for yourself here in Gatlinburg."

Her blue eyes clung to his for a long moment. "You're right, I don't." Her brow furrowed, and she finished her wrap and pushed her empty plate away. "But I've also gotten used to going without the things I want. I live in a crappy trailer, remember?" Her attempt to smile was pathetic.

Another sad admission, which made him want to change things for her. If only she'd shove her independent stubborn streak aside long enough to let him.

Hailey was in the process of taking a sip of her iced tea when someone hit her from behind. The tea sloshed out of the glass, spilling all over, but Rock barely noticed. He was up on his feet and rushing after the guy who'd elbowed her.

"Hey! Hey you! Stop him!" Rock followed the man who now looked larger and older than the guy Hailey had described.

The big man turned to face him. "What's your problem, man?"

Not the knife guy. Rock blew out a breath and raised a hand. "Nothing, sorry. My mistake." Feeling like a complete idiot, he quickly returned to the café where Hailey was mopping up the mess with a napkin.

"I thought that was our knife guy," Rock said sheepishly, coming up to stand beside her. "But I think he bumped into you by accident."

"That's what I assumed," she said dryly. Then the corner of her mouth twitched, and suddenly she burst into laughter. "Oh, if you could have seen your face as you took off after him. I actually felt sorry for the guy."

"Yeah, yeah." Her laughter was nice and infectious enough that he couldn't help but grin. "The damsel in distress was saved from an elbow bump to the back of the head."

Hailey rose to her feet, standing dangerously close to him. "Thanks for being my hero," she said softly, giving him a quick kiss on the cheek and a hug. He gathered her close, reveling in the embrace for several seconds before she pulled away. "Excuse me, but I need to wash up in the bathroom."

Rock nodded, watching her walk inside. The surprising way she'd hugged him gave him hope that Hailey wasn't as immune to him as he'd thought.

For a man who'd sworn off relationships, he spent an inordinate amount of time imagining what it would be like to kiss Hailey Donovan.

# CHAPTER ELEVEN

As Hailey finished drying her T-shirt in the bathroom, she wondered why on earth she'd hugged Rock and kissed his cheek. That sort of casual intimacy wasn't like her, but somehow his determination to be her staunch protector made her want to thank him.

Not to mention, his musky scent was driving her insane. She really needed to try to think of Rock as a friend. Thankfully, she hadn't kissed him the way she'd secretly wanted to. Her cheeks burned at the thought.

And clearly, her less than brilliant plan to draw the knife guy out of hiding wasn't working. The way Rock had taken off after the man who'd bumped into her struck her as funny, but now she knew if the knife guy was watching her, he wouldn't come within arm's length of her while Rock was close by. For one thing, Rock wore his ranger uniform, and he was armed.

Although he'd shot at her twice with Rock right next to her. But that was likely a crime of opportunity, without fear of being caught.

She didn't think he'd use a rifle in downtown Gatlinburg, leaving him with the knife as his only viable option. Shaking Rock loose wouldn't be easy. He'd never let her go without a fight. No matter how tempting it was to slip out the back of the café, she couldn't do it.

Rock thought she deserved better, but she knew that wasn't right. He was the one who deserved the truth. If she had the courage to tell him.

The iced tea stain on her T-shirt didn't look too bad, mostly because her drink had been watered down as the ice melted. Still, she felt self-conscious about her appearance, ragged at best, and now worse so, as she returned to their table.

She sighed when she saw Rock had paid the bill. "You were supposed to let me pay my share."

"No need, it's the least I can do." He rose and reached for her backpack. "Let's go."

She took the pack from him and slung it over her shoulder. "I guess this was a lame idea," she said glumly.

"Not necessarily," Rock said, surprising her. "While rushing after that guy, I thought I caught movement of someone else running away. When I glanced in that direction, though, I didn't see anyone."

"Really?" She wished she'd thought to look around rather than mopping up the mess and worrying about how she looked. Seriously, she was losing her mind around Rock Wilson. The guy made her realize the lukewarm feelings she had toward Jacob were nothing in comparison to the way she felt toward Rock. The ranger crowded into her thoughts more than he should.

Or maybe the truer statement was that she couldn't seem to pry him out of her mind.

Whatever. She turned and walked in the opposite direction from the motel. She couldn't bear to go back there, even if her plan to draw out the knife guy hadn't worked.

Depressing to realize that if she couldn't draw him out, the police likely wouldn't find him either.

"Do you have a destination in mind?" Rock asked, keeping pace beside her.

"Not really." She glanced at him. "I can't sit in that motel room, so it's either wander around town or head over to find a ride out of here." As soon as she uttered the last statement, she winced. "Sorry, never mind, I know I promised to stay twenty-four hours."

"Okay, we'll walk," Rock agreed. "Place is crazy with tourists, though. I hadn't realized how much of a tourist place Gatlinburg turned into over the years."

"Yeah, Pigeon Forge is the same way."

"Been there recently?" he asked idly. "I know the trolley goes back and forth between the two cities."

"Ten years ago, but it was touristy then, I'm sure it's only worse now." Pigeon Forge reminded her of Darby. It was getting harder to believe her foster sister was involved in these attacks. The Darby she knew would have come face-to-face with her, letting Hailey have it.

People changed. Hadn't she? Hailey knew she wasn't the same person she'd been ten years ago. Darby had likely changed too. And she had to face the possibility that her younger sister may not have changed for the better.

She almost prayed that God would look over Darby, then she caught herself. Why would God start looking after any of the foster kids now? He should have been watching over them when the Preacher had been shouting and hitting them with a switch as they kneeled for hours on end.

No matter what Darby was doing now, it had to be better than if they'd stayed with the Preacher.

Which reminded her of Rock's faith. This time, she'd been mentally prepared, so his before meal prayer hadn't upset her. She wouldn't begrudge him his faith, even if she didn't understand it.

Although, deep down, she felt certain if Rock had lived through the horror she had, he wouldn't be so quick to believe.

Rock's cell phone rang. She glanced at him as he drew it from his pocket. He turned the screen to show her that the caller was his boss, and he let the call go to voice mail.

"I meant to ask if you left your friend my phone number so he could call you back?" Rock glanced at her questioningly.

"No, of course not. Why would I do that? It's your phone, not mine." She waved a hand. "In my message, I told him I'd try to get in touch later."

"Okay, although he might try to call you on my phone regardless," Rock said. He gestured to a nearby store. "I think we should pick up a replacement phone for you."

She mentally counted the cash in her pocket and shook her head. "No thanks, it's not a necessity."

A flash of frustration crossed his features. "Would you let me buy one for you?"

"No. You've been feeding me enough as it is, along with paying for the motel room. I can't ask for anything more."

"You didn't ask, I offered." Rock was silent for a few moments, before he added, "To be honest, it would make me feel better to have a way to get in touch with you. The idea of you leaving town and never hearing from you makes me feel sick to my stomach. Those disposable phones like the one that was broken in your trailer aren't expensive. It would mean a lot to me if you'd let me buy one for you."

Put like that, she felt mean and petty for saying no. She

sighed and reluctantly nodded. "Okay, fine. But this is it, then, agreed?"

"Agreed." He steered her toward the discount store. "Thank you."

"I'm the one getting a phone out of the deal," she said dryly. "I should be thanking you."

The purchase didn't take long, and she ultimately agreed to return to the motel in order to activate and power up the thing. It took a while to make the trek back to the motel, and there was still no sign of the guy who'd attacked her.

As she went through the process of getting her phone to work, she had to admit it would be nice to be able to call Nora at some point, to thank her again for everything. Maybe Nora would consider giving her a reference too.

As always, the thought of getting a new job was depressing. There were plenty of lower-level jobs available, those that barely paid a living wage. But she'd waitressed and worked fast food, so she was sure she'd find something similar. Not that she'd loved those jobs. She'd even tried being a receptionist, but she'd hated being stuck indoors.

She'd need to find a place like Nora's hobby farm, where she could spend her days outside and preferably working with animals.

"I have your number programmed into my contact list, please take mine," Rock said. She nodded and punched in the information as he recited the number.

"All set." She slid the phone into her jeans pocket. "If you don't mind, I'm going to head over to the lobby to use the computer for a bit."

"Okay." Rock didn't look thrilled, but he didn't insist on following her either. She was glad to have some time away from him.

All this togetherness was a bit much. She'd never spent this much time with Jacob while they were seeing each other. Which may explain why things had fizzled out after six months.

She slipped out of the motel room and crossed the parking lot to the lobby. Her chances of finding Darby weren't good, but it didn't stop her from trying. And now that she had a phone, she could call Sawyer again too.

Pausing near the doorway, she pulled out her phone and dialed the number to the nonemergency number for the Chattanooga police department. She asked to speak to Sawyer Murphy and almost fell over when he answered.

"Hailey? Is it really you?"

"Sawyer." Ridiculous tears pricked her eyes as she spoke to her foster brother for the first time in thirteen years. "Yeah, it's me. I can't believe you're a cop!"

Sawyer laughed, and it occurred to her that she hadn't heard the sound before now. There hadn't been any laughter in their time with the Preacher. "Yeah, it's a long story. How are you?"

"I'm great, thanks. Have you heard from any of the other fosters? I've lost track of Darby."

"I haven't, although not for lack of trying," Sawyer admitted. "Without last names, it's almost impossible to find a bunch of kids who disappeared into the woods thirteen years ago."

"I know, I only found you because I knew your last name was Murphy. And you obviously kept it."

"How did you remember that?" Sawyer sounded surprised. "I hate to admit I don't know your last name."

"Donovan," she supplied. "But I don't know what name Darby's going by these days. Or Jayme and the others either."

"Me either, but I'll keep trying to find them," Sawyer said.

Neither one of them wanted to admit there was a possibility that some of the kids hadn't survived.

"I may be heading your way," she said, breaking the silence. "If you don't mind having a visitor, I'd love to chat."

"I'd be happy to talk to you, Hailey. I am in the middle of a case, though, so just be prepared that I might not have as much free time as I'd like."

"I understand." Being a cop was important work. Even though she normally avoided law enforcement, she'd make an exception for Sawyer. "It's good to talk to you, Sawyer."

"Same here," he agreed. "Is this your phone number? You called from a different one earlier, right?"

"Yes, that was a friend's phone. This is my number." She humbly knew she had Rock to thank for this connection to her past.

"Okay, I'm making a note of it. Listen, Hailey, I have to go, but please call me if you make it to Chattanooga, okay?"

"I will. Stay safe, Sawyer."

"You too." He disconnected from the line.

She leaned against the side of the motel, thinking about Sawyer's plan to find the others. A cop stood a much better chance than she did.

She was about to go inside when she caught movement from the corner of her eye. A man standing behind the furthest corner of the motel? She instantly took off running in that direction, but when she reached the corner, she stopped abruptly, looking around in disbelief.

Whoever had been there was gone. Yet it seemed clear the knife guy had remained close by, apparently determined to take her out of the equation.

Permanently.

ROCK HAPPENED to see Hailey run past the motel window and quickly threw open the door to join in the chase. He met up with her at the far corner of the motel.

"What happened?" he demanded.

"I thought I saw knife guy," she said with a grimace. "But by the time I got here, he was gone."

"He knows where we're staying," Rock said grimly. "That's a problem."

"Depends on how you look at it," Hailey pointed out. "My plan to bait him out of hiding worked. Sort of."

Every fiber of his being hated her plan, but he didn't voice his concern. She already knew where he stood on the subject. "We should let Sergeant Kellen know about this."

"Maybe he can get someone to watch the place, wait for knife guy to show up again?" Hailey suggested.

"It's possible." He glanced at her, already knowing she wouldn't go along with his idea but determined to put it out there anyway. "I'd feel better if we could stay inside our rooms for the rest of the night."

"It's barely four o'clock in the afternoon, I'm not sitting inside for that long," she protested.

"For now," he amended. "Until I connect with Kellen."

"Fine." Hailey turned and walked toward her room. He stopped her and gently guided her to his doorway.

"Just in case he's watching," he murmured in a low voice.

Hailey didn't argue. She slipped inside once he'd unlocked the door. He quickly called Kellen but was forced to leave a message.

"I think we should walk around some more," Hailey said. "At least we know he's out there."

"You got a clear look at him?" Rock asked.

"Not really, but who else would it be?"

"I don't know, yet I already chased one innocent man, and for all we know that guy was sneaking back there to smoke."

"He wouldn't run if that was the case."

"Let's just wait until Kellen calls me back before we head out." He wasn't above trying to buy some time. "Did you find what you were looking for on the computer?"

"I never went into the lobby, I stood outside and spoke with my friend Sawyer instead." A hint of a smile played on her features, and he battled yet another wave of jealousy at the man who'd put it there. "Thanks for the phone, Rock. It was really nice to talk to Sawyer after all these years, and I couldn't have done that without you."

The mystery friend had a name, Sawyer. He forced a smile. "You're welcome. Does this mean you're heading out to visit him tomorrow?"

"Maybe." She shrugged. "Although if the man I saw was the knife guy, I'd rather stick around long enough to get him into custody."

"Me too." He pulled out his phone, willing Kellen to return his call. "If you're set on taking a walk, let's go to the police department. From there, we'll wander around until we find a place to eat dinner."

"Okay." Hailey eagerly headed for the door.

Rock kept a keen eye out for any sign that the motel was being watched. He didn't see anyone lurking nearby but wondered if the knife guy was sitting somewhere with a pair of binoculars, waiting for an opportunity to strike.

After hearing Hailey had stood outside to use the phone, it made sense the guy had been close enough to come toward her.

The only good thing about that was that he likely wasn't lugging a rifle around town. If he wanted to attack Hailey, he'd have to get up close and personal.

Rock wanted nothing more than to stick to her like a burr, but she wasn't exactly cooperating.

At the police station, Sergeant Kellen looked harried. "Lots of theft today, my officers are a bit stretched. I can try to get someone to watch the motel, but no guarantees they'll be sitting there twenty-four seven."

"Understood. Any leads on the thefts?"

"No." Kellen scowled. "If tourists would just carry their money closer to their person, the thieves wouldn't find it so easy to steal from them."

Hailey shifted from one foot to the other, glancing around as if uncomfortable. Rock took the hint. "Okay, thanks for anything you can do to find this guy."

"Of course. We'll do our best. Arresting someone for attempted assault with a deadly weapon is better than pulling in a few pickpockets," Kellen agreed.

"Thanks." It was all Rock could ask for. He led the way outside, Hailey hot on his heels. "Should we head in the opposite direction than we took this morning?"

She nodded, falling into step beside him. "You know, some pickpockets are just trying to survive."

He glanced down at her, sensing she was talking about herself more than the ones stealing from tourists. "I know."

She kicked a pebble. "When you're hungry, I mean really hungry, taking money from those who seem to have more than enough doesn't feel like stealing."

His heart squeezed in his chest. He hated thinking of a young version of Hailey stealing to eat. To survive. "I understand. I haven't been in that position, but I'm sure I'd do the same thing."

She hunched her shoulders as if embarrassed to have said so much. "Yeah, well, not all cops think that way."

He took a chance and lightly wrapped his arm around her shoulders, hugging her close. "I think you're an amazing woman, Hailey Donovan. You're strong, smart, and probably the most hardworking person I've ever met."

She rested against him for a long moment, before straightening. "I'm nothing special. I just did what was necessary to survive."

"Which is very admirable," he insisted.

"I—was in a terrible foster home for five years." Her voice was so low he had to bend down to hear her. "I was one of seven kids, and the second oldest. Well, technically third oldest as Sawyer had me beat by a couple of months."

Sawyer was one of her foster siblings? All previous feelings of jealousy vanished. Rock was fiercely glad she'd been able to connect with one of her foster siblings. "I'm sorry to hear that it was so awful."

She didn't say anything for several minutes. He thought she was finished talking about her past when she said, "One night there was a fire. We were in the cellar and might have burned to death if I hadn't smelled smoke and woken the others. Somehow, we managed to escape. We disappeared into the mountains and never went back."

Her story was heartrending and explained a lot. "I'm glad you found a home and a job here in Gatlinburg."

She shrugged. "I escaped with my younger sister, Darby. She was twelve at the time. But we lost touch, and I haven't seen her in ten years."

That must be who she was searching for on the computer. "I can help you find her," he offered.

She shook her head. "I don't know what name she's using these days. I introduced her to everyone as my sister

Darby Donovan, but I can't even tell you what her real last name is."

"Really?" He found that strange.

"I know it sounds crazy, but you have to understand we were just kids. Kids who were trapped in a nightmare. When we did find time to talk to each other, it was mostly about how to escape, not details about our lives before we ended up with the Preacher."

"The Preacher?" he echoed before he could stop himself. "The one you mentioned yesterday? He actually kept you and the other foster kids in the cellar?"

She let out a sound that sounded like a harsh laugh. "Yes. He preached about God, but we all knew he was the devil himself."

Rock felt as if he'd been sucker punched in the gut. Under those circumstances, he couldn't blame Hailey for not believing in God.

And now he had yet another reason he desperately needed her to stay in Gatlinburg. There was evil in the world, as she knew firsthand, but there was also good. Lots of good. And he felt certain that given time, he might be able to help her see that.

Until then, he silently prayed to find a way to lead Hailey to God's ever-enduring love and support.

# CHAPTER TWELVE

Hailey had no idea why she'd spilled her guts to Rock. After dating Jacob for several months, she hadn't confided to him about her past. Clearly another indication that their so-called relationship was doomed.

Oddly enough, telling Rock about the Preacher brought a sense of relief. She was secretly stunned at his unwavering support. He was smart enough to realize she'd gotten into trouble for stealing and hadn't made her feel bad about what she'd done.

She was starting to realize that Rock was a unique guy. A man who loved the outdoors as much as she did, who accepted her despite her numerous flaws, and who was extremely easy to be around.

No wonder she was finding it hard to leave Gatlinburg. Even knowing Sawyer was in Chattanooga wasn't enough to send her sprinting out of town. The way she should be.

Oh, she wanted to visit her foster brother, there was no doubt about that. But *visit* was the operative word.

Moving to Chattanooga, finding a place to live and a new job, wasn't high on her list of fun things to do. In the past five years, she'd worked for Nora, and she hadn't taken more than a couple of days off, mostly to move from a lousy apartment to an equally lousy trailer or simply to spend a long weekend hiking and enjoying nature.

If she was able to stay in Gatlinburg, she felt certain Nora would give her time off to visit Sawyer. Maybe after the tourist season when things weren't so busy. As a cop, Sawyer would also be busy with the influx of tourists.

"Hailey, there isn't anything I can say to make up for what you've been through," Rock said softly. "But I want you to know I'm here for you. I'm willing to listen any time you need to talk. No judgment."

"Thanks, Rock. I haven't told anyone about my past," she confessed. "I'd rather bury the memories, but that hasn't been working well."

"How often do you have nightmares about him?"

"Not as much anymore," she admitted. "It might have been triggered by sleeping on the floor in the cabin. I was out of practice, I guess."

She felt Rock's muscles tense with anger, but his tone remained mild. "I hope once you were safe, you reported him to the police."

"No need, the Preacher and his wife, Ruth, didn't escape the fire."

"Too bad, I would rather he rot in prison for the rest of his life." Rock scowled.

She didn't say anything because voicing her thoughts out loud about how a devil belonged in a pit of fire probably wouldn't sound good.

Especially to a believer like Rock.

They walked in silence for several moments. She could tell Rock had lots of questions, but she had to give him brownie points for not prying.

"No sign of knife guy," she murmured, changing the subject. "I was really hoping he'd come after me again."

"You do realize how nuts that sounds, right?" Rock asked wryly.

She had to smile. "I guess, but not knowing when he'll show up is worse."

"The police will pick him up," Rock assured her. "Especially now that they know he's watching the motel."

"Yeah." She didn't have Rock's level of faith, but that was nothing new. Since escaping the Preacher, she'd depended solely on herself, caring for Darby as best she could.

Until now. There was no denying that she wouldn't be walking around Gatlinburg without Rock's support and assistance.

She really hoped he wouldn't lose his job over her.

"Are you hungry?" He gestured to another restaurant offering outdoor seating. "I hear the food is decent at the Starlight Inn."

"Looks expensive," she murmured. "I can just grab a burger and meet you back at the motel."

"Not happening," Rock said firmly. "I know you're trying to put distance between us to draw knife guy out, but I'm not leaving you. If you want burgers, that's fine with me. I just thought you'd enjoy sitting outside."

She would enjoy that, but she didn't want to waste her money on an expensive meal. Food was necessary to survive, but in her mind, the cheaper the better. "We can get burgers and find a picnic table, which is basically the same thing."

He chuckled and shook his head. "They're only the same to you, Hailey. Not to most women."

"I know." She knew Rock was about to offer once again

to pay for her meal, but she wasn't going to let him do that. It wasn't as if they were dating, and he'd done more than enough for her already.

Driving her to town, providing meals, and paying motel costs, not to mention warning her of the knife guy in time to save her life.

If she didn't know better, she'd think God had sent Rock to watch over her.

"Interested in any place in particular?" Rock asked, breaking into her thoughts.

"Wasn't there a place we passed earlier that had outdoor seating?" She frowned trying to remember. "This way." She gestured to the left.

"Works for me," Rock agreed. They walked for another thirty minutes before finding the restaurant she remembered. She pounced on an empty table before anyone else could snatch it up. "Do you want to get your food first?"

"Sure. Wait here." Rock hurried inside, leaving her sitting at the table alone.

Glancing around, she secretly hoped the knife guy would come rushing toward her. But, of course, he didn't. In what seemed like record time, Rock returned with a tray full of food. She scowled.

"Do not tell me you bought two meals."

"Okay, I won't tell you, but I did." His hazel eyes gleamed with satisfaction. "You may as well help me eat this, or it will go to waste."

"Rock . . ." She sighed. "You promised I could pay my own way."

"I don't think it was a promise so much as I didn't argue with your statement," he pointed out. "And really, Hailey, you should save your money just in case you need to leave town. I have more than enough to cover the food and the motel."

"That's not the point." She was super irritated and couldn't quite explain why. Back in those early days, she'd have taken any free meal without blinking an eye. "You earned your money, and I'm not a broke charity case."

"Never said you were." Rock picked up a burger, unwrapped it, and took a bite. He chewed for a few moments, then swallowed. "Here's what you don't seem to understand. It's more fun buying you food because of your independent attitude. I know you're not expecting it, and it makes me happy to give you these small things. I already told you how much I admire you, Hailey. You're the strongest, most independent woman I know. Now pipe down and eat your food before it gets cold."

Pipe down? What, was she ten? Then again, the enticing scent of french fries made it difficult to stay mad. Her fingers inched forward and stole one of the fries. She inwardly sighed, knowing it was her own fault. If she'd have been thinking clearly, she should have made him sit there so she could go in first.

Instead, she'd focused on drawing out knife guy.

"This is the last meal you're buying for me, understand?" Grumpily, she took the other burger and opened it.

Rock nodded but didn't say anything, which only told her that he'd try the same thing come breakfast the following morning.

She didn't want to admire his persistence. And he thought she was stubborn? He was worse than Rory the donkey. The thought made her smile.

"Does that mean I'm forgiven?" Rock asked.

"What?" Then she understood. "No, actually, in my mind I was renaming Rory the donkey *Rock*."

He threw his head back and laughed. His laughter was so contagious she joined in.

"That's hilarious because in my mind, I've been renaming Rory the donkey *Hailey*." Rock let out another burst of laughter.

"Copycat." Hailey wiped tears from her eyes and resumed eating. As Rock mentioned, no sense in letting good food go to waste.

Rock's phone rang again. With a frown, he pulled it out, glanced at the screen, then quickly answered it. "This is Ranger Wilson. Do you have news, Sergeant?"

She froze, her french fry halfway to her mouth. Had they caught knife guy? Was it possible this weird nightmare was over?

Not that these past twenty-four hours had been nearly as difficult to get through as those years with the Preacher.

"We'll be there in twenty." Rock disconnected from the line. "They have a man in custody, but fair warning, he doesn't look very much like your sketch. And the partial fingerprint doesn't match either. But they caught him trying to steal a knife, so they decided to see if they could get him to confess."

Reading his gaze, she already knew. "But he didn't."

"No. But they'd like you to participate in looking at a set of six mug shots to see if you can identify him." Rock shrugged. "It can't hurt."

"Yeah, okay." Her earlier excitement vanished. It was easy to follow the cop's logic. If knife guy had lost his weapon, why not try to steal a replacement.

Yet if he didn't look like her sketch or match the partial fingerprint, she didn't have a lot of hope he was the right guy. Her glimpse had been brief, but there was still a grainy image firmly implanted in her mind. Although it was possible the baseball cap had covered his head and hair enough to have skewed the sketch.

"Take your time in finishing your dinner," Rock advised. "It's going to take the police a little time to get their mug shots together."

She relaxed and ate another fry. "Understandable."

They finished eating, took care of their garbage, then walked back toward the police station. Even though they had a man in custody, Hailey kept a sharp eye out for anyone looking suspicious.

If they did have the right man, she wondered if he'd implicate Darby in any way. Now, she wished she'd kept her mouth shut about the foster kids, especially Darby.

When they reached the police station, she reminded herself not to think the worst. All she really knew about Darby was that her younger sister had left town while Hailey had been locked up in juvie.

Rock held the door for her. When she crossed the threshold, she saw Morrison coming toward her. Rock quickly stepped in front of her.

"Get outta my way," Morrison growled, brushing past them.

Rock moved just enough to allow the guy to leave. Easy to see Morrison blamed them for his recent desk duty, which was partially accurate. She was still secretly surprised Rock had gone over the guy's head.

If she'd have tried that, she doubted Sergeant Kellen would have listened.

While Rock locked up his weapon, Kellen approached. "Have a seat in the interview room, we'll bring the photos in a few minutes," Kellen instructed.

She followed Rock into the windowless room and

wiped her damp, nervous palms on her jeans. "I really hope it's him," she murmured.

"Me too." Rock held her gaze. "Don't give up hope if it's not," he added. "They'll find him."

She nodded, wishing she believed him. The minutes passed with excruciating slowness, until Kellen returned, holding a paper with six faces on it. "Okay, I want you to look at each face here and see if you recognize him. Take your time, we don't want any mistakes."

Drawing a deep breath, she nodded. Peering down at the mug shots, she studied each face, comparing it to the mental picture she had in her head.

By the time she got to the last one, she was hit by a wave of frustration. "I'm sorry, but none of these men look familiar. The man who tried to stab me isn't among them."

"Are you sure?" Kellen pressed. "Imagine them wearing a baseball cap."

Dutifully, she did as he suggested, but it was no use. Her assailant wasn't here. "I'm sorry," she repeated. "I wish he was there, but he's not."

It was disheartening to accept that the man who'd stabbed her was still out there, somewhere. Waiting for another opportunity to strike.

---

ROCK HAD BEEN afraid of this, but he didn't let his disappointment show. Hailey was doing her best. And from what he could tell, these guys didn't resemble her sketch at all.

"Okay, well, it was worth a shot." Kellen's tone was dejected. "We appreciate you coming in."

"Are you still going to test his DNA, just in case?" Rock asked.

Hailey looked annoyed. "It's not him, Rock. No sense in wasting time and money."

He wasn't about to point out that no one was infallible. He trusted in Hailey's ability to identify the guy, but as Kellen pointed out, the guy had been wearing a hat. Her memory may not be 100 percent on point.

Hailey jumped up and moved toward the door. Rock stood, glancing at Sergeant Kellen. "Which one is he?"

Kellen grimaced and pointed to the guy in the middle of the bottom row. "I should have known it was a long shot, especially since the print didn't match."

"You did the right thing by asking us to come in," Rock said. "Thanks for that. Oh, and I'd really like you to find a way to have a cop sit on our motel," he reminded him. "Hailey's pretty sure she caught a glimpse of him hanging out there."

"Yeah, I'll see what I can do," Kellen groused.

He flashed a sympathetic smile. After retrieving his weapon, he followed Hailey outside. Without hesitating, she turned and walked in the opposite direction from the motel.

"What's your plan, Hailey?" he asked after several moments of silence.

"I really want to find this guy." Her tone was laced with frustration. "He's out here, somewhere, it shouldn't be this difficult to spot him."

There wasn't anything he could say in response. "I know you only agreed to stay until the morning, but if he is hanging around town, you could postpone your departure another day."

She glared at him without saying anything. Based on

how upset she'd been at his buying her dinner, he sensed it was lack of money preventing her from sticking around for another day.

It was frustrating because he didn't mind helping her out. He wanted this guy arrested just as much as she did. And he also knew the guy wasn't going to come out of hiding to attack her while he was standing right there.

It was obvious Hailey knew it too.

"Let's just go back to the stupid motel." She came to an abrupt stop. "There's no point in wandering aimlessly around for the rest of the evening."

The sky was still fairly light as the summer solstice approached. He nodded. "Whatever you want, Hailey."

She glanced at him. "Do you know which of those men was the one they'd arrested for stealing the knife?"

He hesitated, then nodded. "Middle of the bottom row."

She shook her head. "The guy I saw at the bus depot was definitely older. Those guys were all in their late twenties, maybe early thirties."

He'd noticed that, too, and wished he'd gotten a better look at the guy. "I know. But the fact that he tried to steal a knife made it important to rule him out as a suspect."

"They're still going to run the DNA, aren't they?"

He wasn't going to lie to her. "Probably. But don't think of it as a waste of time and money. For one thing, we don't even know if the baseball cap belongs to knife guy. And secondly, a lack of a DNA comparison only reinforces what you told them all along, that he's not the guy."

"Still a waste," she muttered.

Her pragmatic attitude made him grin. No one would ever accuse Hailey of being high maintenance, that was for sure.

Her steps slowed as they approached their side-by-side

motel rooms. He could tell she didn't like being cooped up inside.

"Hailey." He put a hand on her arm to stop her, gently turning her so she faced him. "I know I sound like a broken record, but I want you to stay. Please. For me, and for Nora, and even for Rory."

The corner of her mouth kicked up in a half smile. "I miss the animals like crazy," she said in a low voice. "I hope I can find another job that allows me to work with animals. I tend to do better with four-legged creatures than with people."

"You don't need another job, just stay here long enough for the police to catch this guy." Placing the tip of his finger beneath her chin, he forced her to look at him. "Please, Hailey? For me?"

She stared deep into his eyes as if she might actually agree. He could tell she wanted to stay, it was only her pride and lack of funds holding her back.

Then she surprised him by lifting up on her tiptoes to kiss him. Not on the cheek this time, but on the mouth.

He froze for a second, then urged her closer, deepening the kiss. Her lips were soft, her kiss tentative as if she wasn't sure what she was doing.

He wanted nothing more than to deepen the kiss, but he was afraid of scaring her. She hadn't mentioned any sexual assault in her past, but that didn't mean it hadn't happened.

She pulled away, ending their kiss far too soon. It took a moment for his brain cells to fire on all synapses.

"Hailey, does that mean you'll stay?" He feared it was more likely a kiss goodbye.

A loud crack of gunfire made him jump. He ducked and dragged Hailey down to the ground with him. He frantically searched for his room key so they could get inside.

Hailey must have had her key in hand because she managed to get her door open first. She practically fell inside, and he crawled forward, following her.

He quickly shut the door, locked it, then reached for his phone. "The cops better have seen that," he said grimly.

Hailey didn't answer, her eyes wide with shock. "I—think the bullet hit the wall between us."

"You do?" Of course, Sergeant Kellen didn't answer, the guy had probably already gone home. He called the emergency number, demanding officers respond to an active shooter.

"I saw the bullet hole in the side of the motel," Hailey said, her expression dazed. "It was right where my head had been."

He swallowed a lump of regret. He shouldn't have dismissed the possibility of this guy using a gun in town.

Because it was clear he had. And by the time the cops arrived, Rock had no doubt he'd be long gone.

# CHAPTER THIRTEEN

*The guy was a lousy shot*, Hailey thought as she twisted her hands together to stop them from trembling. This had been his third attempt to shoot her, and he'd missed every time.

Grateful as she was, it was curious. Why keep shooting if you can't hit what you're aiming at? Was this some sort of amateur gunman?

"This is my fault, I shouldn't have assumed he wouldn't use his rifle in town," Rock said in a self-deprecating tone.

"I'm pretty sure it's the shooter's fault," she said mildly. "And mine, since I offered myself up as bait to draw him out."

"I only let you do that because I figured he'd stick to using a knife," Rock shot back.

"Let me?" The spurt of anger helped calm her nerves. "Pretty sure I can make my own decisions, thanks."

Rock lowered his head and rubbed the back of his neck. "I know you can," he finally said, lifting his gaze to hers. "But you have to admit that attempt was too close."

"Actually, I was thinking he was a lousy shot." She unwrapped her fingers, pleased to see the trembling had subsided. "He's zero for three with the rifle. He'd gotten much closer with the knife."

"Or maybe God is watching over you," Rock said. "And I'm grateful for it."

"Yeah, right." Her response was automatic, but deep down, she couldn't help but wonder if there was a kernel of truth to his belief. Although if there was truly a God who was watching over her, then why now?

Why not when she'd been a scared nine-year-old sent to the Preacher's cabin of horrors in the woods?

"Hailey, there is always good in the world, to balance out the evil," Rock said softly. "If the devil exists, then there has to be a God to counter him. Otherwise, we'd all be doomed."

She frowned, his words resonating in spite of herself. Because he was right about there being good in the world. Nora was wonderful, and Rock wasn't too bad himself.

Still, it was difficult to let go of the past.

Before she could respond, there was a knock at the door. "Gatlinburg police! Are you okay?"

"We're not hurt," Rock called back, rising to his feet and opening the door. The two uniformed officers weren't familiar. Hailey was glad Morrison had been taken off the case.

"Have you found any sign of him?" Rock asked.

The two officers looked at each other, and Hailey knew they hadn't before one of them admitted, "No."

Rock muttered something harsh under his breath as he turned away. Oddly, she wanted to comfort him.

"There's a slug embedded in the motel room wall," she said, moving toward the door.

The officers stepped back to allow her to pass. She swallowed hard when she looked at the small dark hole in the wood, so close to where they'd been kissing.

*Kissing!*

"Here," she said, her voice sounding strange to her own ears.

One of the officers used his radio to call for a crime scene tech. "Thanks, we'll get that slug out of there, see if we can figure out what the make and model of the rifle this guy is using."

She nodded, crossing her arms over her chest. It was another small piece of evidence, but unlikely to be of much use unless they found the weapon.

And the man who'd used it.

"We'll need to take your statement, Ms. Donovan," one of the officers said. She looked at his name tag.

"I know, Officer Perkins." She forced a smile. The other cop had already gone inside with Rock.

Moving through the connecting door, she sat at the small table. Officer Perkins took out a small notebook.

Her statement was brief because there wasn't much she could offer. No, she hadn't seen anything. She'd heard the gunshot and hit the ground, then managed to unlock the motel room door and fall inside, with Rock following close behind.

"You're sure you don't know who is behind these attacks?" Officer Perkins pressed.

It was the same question over and over. From Rock, Morrison, Sergeant Kellen, and now Officer Perkins. "Don't you think I'd tell you if I did?" she snapped, losing her temper. "It's not like I'm enjoying being used as target practice by this guy over the past forty-eight hours."

"I'm sorry, ma'am," Perkins said without looking the least bit apologetic. "You have to understand that most repeated attacks like this are personal in nature."

She bit back another sarcastic response. Of course, it

was personal, but she didn't know who or why. "As I told Sergeant Kellen and Officer Morrison, my former boyfriend Jacob Rokeby left me for another woman, so I can't imagine he's behind this. I don't have any other enemies that I'm aware of." She frowned. "Haven't they checked Jacob's alibi by now?"

"I'm not sure," Perkins said evasively. "Do you have anything else to add?"

"No. I wish I did," she added bitterly.

"Okay, thanks, Ms. Donovan." Perkins closed his little notebook and rose to his feet. Outside the motel room, she could hear the crime scene tech prying the bullet out of the wall.

"Have you spoken to Sergeant Kellen about this?" Rock asked, joining them.

Perkins shook his head, glancing at the other officer standing behind Rock as if seeking reassurance. "No, he'll be debriefed in the morning."

Rock scowled. "I'll call him myself, then. Wasn't there an officer watching the motel?"

Again, the two cops exchanged a long look. "Officer Brown was sitting on the motel, but he was called away for an attempted robbery."

"Another tourist, I assume," Rock said on a sigh.

"Yeah," Perkins confirmed. "But Gatlinburg would be a ghost town without them."

It was a fancy way of saying the tourists ultimately paid the cops' salaries. And she couldn't argue since Nora's hobby farm wouldn't exist without tourists either.

The cops left, leaving her and Rock standing awkwardly in the room. The kiss seemed to loom in the air between them.

"I, uh, need to get some rest," she finally said.

"Hailey," Rock said as she turned away. She inwardly winced, hoping he wasn't about to broach the subject of their kiss.

The kiss she'd initiated. Why had she done such a crazy thing?

"What?" she asked, glancing at him over her shoulder.

"Will you please consider staying another day?" When she opened her mouth to respond, he held up his hand. "No, don't say anything now, just think about it. We have the slug and your sketch. If they do find someone to arrest, they'll make you come back to do either a lineup or another photo array."

She hadn't considered that, but she wasn't ready to make a commitment to stay either. "I'll think about it," she said softly. "Good night, Rock."

"Good night, Hailey." He moved through the connecting doorway to his room.

She cleaned up in the bathroom, then crawled into bed. But sleep didn't come easily.

Memories of kissing Rock, and the way he'd kissed her back, played over and over in her mind like a movie loop.

Worst of all? She longed to be held in his arms, to experience that closeness again.

And if that wasn't enough to convince her to leave town, nothing would.

---

ROCK STARED up at the ceiling, trying to come up with additional arguments that might sway Hailey into staying. Even though he knew better than to think she'd do anything other than exactly what she wanted.

Remembering how she'd compared him to Rory the

donkey made him smile. Her kiss had shocked him, but he'd take that kind of surprise any day of the week.

He finally fell asleep but woke abruptly, feeling disoriented. Had he heard something? Her motel room door closing?

Jackknifing off the bed, he rushed to the connecting door. Her side was open, and his heart squeezed painfully.

But then he noticed the bathroom door was closed and her backpack was still sitting on the floor beside the bed. He felt his entire body sag in relief.

She hadn't left. *Yet.*

He made quick use of his own bathroom, grimacing at the state of his uniform. He needed something different to wear, and soon.

Or his body odor alone would drive Hailey straight to finding a taxi.

When he emerged from the bathroom, he pulled up short when he saw Hailey sitting in the corner of his room with to-go bags of breakfast sandwiches.

Of course, she'd bought breakfast. He couldn't help but grin. "Thanks for the meal, that was nice of you."

"My turn, right?" she said lightly.

"Do you always keep score?" He crossed over to join her.

When her smile faded, he wished he could take the statement back. "No."

"I'm sorry, that didn't come out the way I intended." He wished he dared to give her a hug. "It just seems like you don't want to owe anyone anything."

She took a bite of her bacon, egg, and cheese sandwich. "I guess that's fair. I know you're not the type to cash in favors in exchange for meals, but old habits are hard to break."

He froze in the act of unwrapping his sandwich, registering what she was saying. It made him sick to know how vulnerable she must have been in those early years. "Never, Hailey." His voice was low and rough. "Everything I've done for you has been out of caring for your welfare, nothing more." Then a horrible realization struck him. "That's not why you kissed me last night, is it?"

"No," she said firmly, her cheeks pink. "I honestly don't know what possessed me to do that."

"Hey, I'm not saying I didn't enjoy it." He flashed a cheeky grin, trying to lighten the mood. "Feel free to kiss me anytime, just not because you think you owe me. Because you don't."

She rolled her eyes and took another bite of her sandwich. Then she set it down. "Sorry, I know you like to pray before eating."

He was touched by her offer, especially considering her stance on God and faith. "I think God will forgive us; it's what He does best."

She stared down at her sandwich for a long moment. Then she raised her gaze to his. "There might be some merit to your good vs. evil theory."

"Of course, I'm right," he teased.

She didn't smile. "I guess I'm just trying to understand why some people have to deal with so much evil as compared to others. Especially kids."

The bit of food he'd ingested sat like a lump in his gut. It was a fair question, one he couldn't answer. "I don't know, Hailey. I wish I knew why some people suffer so much more so than others. When I lost both of my parents right out of high school, I was angry at God because I couldn't understand why He'd taken them from me."

She reached over and lightly touched his hand. "I'm

sorry for your loss. I don't have any real memories of my parents. Only my mother leaving me home alone and hungry, which is how I ended up in foster care."

He couldn't imagine what she'd been through. "My loss was nothing compared to yours. And yet there are plenty of others who seem to have everything they want and then some. I've come to accept that God doesn't want us to compare ourselves to others. I think He wants us to believe in Him, to have faith in Him, and to trust in His plan for us." He stopped, flushing at the way he sounded like a preacher.

Something Hailey wouldn't hardly appreciate, given her past experience with a man who was about as far from God as a man could get.

He thought about apologizing, but she seemed to be considering his words. "Not comparing yourself to others is difficult," she admitted. "I guess I didn't realize how much resentment I still have bottled up inside."

Turning his hand beneath hers, he clasped her fingers warmly in his. "Hailey, if anyone deserves a bit of resentment, it's you. But hanging on to those feelings will only hold you back. You need to let go of the past if you want to move forward and have a future."

She looked at their clasped hands for a moment, then met his gaze. "You make it sound easy."

"I know it's not," he countered.

The corner of her mouth tipped up in a smile. "I'll try."

"Good." He reluctantly released her hand to resume eating.

When they finished their meal, he cleaned away the garbage and made more coffee in the small coffeepot on the dresser.

"I'll stay another day," Hailey announced.

"I'm happy to hear that." He beamed, unable to contain his joy and relief. "I know we're close to getting this guy."

"I hope so, it's the main reason I'm sticking around." She glanced around the motel room. "Not these luxury accommodations. Which are only slightly nicer than my trailer even before it was trashed."

"I'll help you clean up your trailer, after we find this guy."

She waved a dismissive hand. "I can do it. You've helped more than enough."

"No keeping score," he scolded. Then he grimaced and reached into his pocket for his phone. "I almost forgot, I need to call my boss."

Hailey opened her mouth to say something, but then stopped herself. She helped herself to a cup of coffee, then filled a cup for him.

Thankfully, his boss didn't answer the phone, which meant Rock could leave a message. He hated making the rest of the team short-staffed, especially in the middle of summer, but keeping Hailey alive was more important than tracking poachers.

Sipping his coffee, he eyed Hailey over the rim. "I know you don't want to sit in the motel room all day, but we need to be careful. I'd prefer to be surrounded by people."

"I was just thinking that this guy seems to only shoot at me when I'm either alone or with you." She hesitated, then said, "Maybe helping Nora on the hobby farm wouldn't endanger the kids."

He wanted to reject her idea, but as long as she was sticking around Gatlinburg, why argue? "The only vandalism was to your truck, so it's possible this guy draws the line at hurting kids. Have you spoken to Nora?"

"No. I left a message, but at the time I didn't have a

phone number she could use to call me back." She pulled out her small disposable phone. "I'll try her now, see what she thinks. If she'd rather I wait until this guy is caught, that's fine too."

Rock knew Nora cared about Hailey. Yet she also had a business to run. Personally, he wouldn't take the risk.

He listened as Hailey left Nora a message, briefly explaining she was in danger but was still in Gatlinburg with Rock. She disconnected after leaving Nora her new disposable phone number in case she wanted to call back.

No doubt Nora Rhodes was working from dawn to dusk managing all the chores on her own. By the tortured expression on Hailey's face, she was imagining the same scenario.

"Hey, let's play some mini golf," he suggested. "There should be enough of a crowd to keep the shooter away."

"Okay." She looked hesitant. "I hope you're right about the crowds keeping him away."

"I know he braved the crowds at the trolley station, but I doubt he'd try that a second time." Rock pursed his lips. No one claimed this guy had any logic. The thought of some innocent person being injured or killed because of him made him feel sick to his stomach.

Yet looking back over the past forty-eight hours, the only times he'd risked aiming a gun and shooting at them was when they were alone and away from other people. Was that why he'd brought a knife to the bus station?

Maybe the assailant didn't really want to hurt innocent people.

Well, except maybe for Rock himself. He'd been close enough to have been hit by a stray bullet more than once. Which kind of blew that theory right out of the water.

"Are you ready go to go?" He infused cheerfulness into his tone.

She nodded and darted into her room for a moment, returning with her key. "You'll have to teach me," she said as they headed outside.

"Teach you what? To play mini golf?" He stared at her. "Are you saying you've never played?"

"That's exactly what I'm saying." She stood outside their doorway for a moment, looking at the spot where the bullet had been removed. Then she slowly turned, raking her gaze over the horizon in the most likely direction the shot had come from. "Maybe we should take a walk first. See if we can find something the locals missed."

He couldn't blame her for not trusting the local cops. They hadn't exactly done a stellar job solving her case so far. But he still preferred to stay in the midst of the tourists rather than going off on their own.

"All right," he reluctantly agreed. He followed her gaze, trying to pinpoint the most reasonable spot a shooter might choose. "Where do you want to go?"

"I've been thinking about how this guy keeps missing me. I mean, sure, he gets close, but he hasn't hit his target. Do you think that's because his scope is off? Or is he shooting from too far away?"

"If he was too far away, his shot would be lower," he said thoughtfully. "Especially if he's using a common hunting rifle like the thirty-aught-six. The accuracy of that rifle drops significantly when the target is more than three hundred yards away."

"It's more likely his scope or simply his level of skill, then," Hailey said thoughtfully. "Three hundred yards puts him somewhere up on that hill over there." She gestured with her hand.

*Good eye,* he thought with a sigh. That's exactly where he'd have put the guy too. He pulled his binoculars off his utility belt and peered at the hill. There was nothing out of the ordinary. "Okay, let's check it out."

As they began walking, he tried to keep himself in front of Hailey, protecting her the best he could. Rock was braced for another attack, but as time passed and they grew closer to the wooded hill, he realized if the shooter was smart, he'd be long gone.

The hill was bigger than it looked at nearly three hundred yards away. Finding any sort of clue would be impossible, yet it was all they had to go on.

Rock prayed for strength and wisdom as they began the climb uphill. He'd been so preoccupied with keeping Hailey safe that he almost missed it.

"Rock, look! He was here! Right here!" Hailey ran over to a rocky outcropping, where the sun reflected off the gleam of brass.

A shell casing. He knelt beside it and turned to look through the binoculars again.

The motel, and specifically their two rooms, were dead ahead.

Hailey was right, the shooter had been here. It was a miracle they'd found the shell casing, and he felt certain God had guided them to this spot.

As great as it was to have another clue, they were no closer to figuring out who this guy was and locking him up behind bars.

Where he belonged.

## CHAPTER FOURTEEN

Hailey watched as Rock pulled out a small plastic bag, and using the bag as a glove, he carefully placed the shell casing inside without touching it. She realized it was a good thing he was still wearing his park ranger uniform and utility belt. Rangers must need to pick up evidence from poachers, and the binoculars had come in handy, even though his being armed was likely why the assailant hadn't come after her with a knife while Rock was at her side.

Despite his dirt-stained and wrinkled clothing, she still thought he was the most handsome guy she'd ever met.

Deep down, she knew part of the reason she'd decided to stay another day was because of Rock. She liked him, and for the first time since Jacob had dumped her, she thought it was possible she might actually give another relationship a try. Rock was so different from anyone she knew. His caring compassion was humbling.

When he'd accused her of keeping score, she'd hated to admit he was right. She had purposefully gone out early to get breakfast, partially to see if the assailant would come after her, but mostly because she'd longed to even the scales. To pay for at least one of their meals.

Truthfully, she'd never considered that keeping score made her come across as petty.

Maybe she was Rory the donkey.

"I hope they can lift a print off this that will match the one on the knife," Rock said, interrupting her thoughts. "If so, that will prove the shooter and the knife guy are one and the same."

"I'm surprised he didn't pick it up before leaving." She glanced around the wooded area, thinking once again that this guy wasn't very smart.

Not that she was complaining about his ineptness. The more clues they had to nail him with, the better.

"It was getting dark when he took the shot," Rock said thoughtfully. "And he probably panicked when he realized he missed his target, especially after we managed to get to safety inside the motel room."

She could see Rock's point. "Still, this all seems"—she waved a hand—"I don't know, amateurish."

Rock shook his head. "Not that much of an amateur." He pinned her with his hazel gaze. "Think about how close it was. If you hadn't broken off our kiss when you had, he'd have hit you."

Her cheeks burned at the mention of their kiss. "Or you," she countered, hating the thought of Rock being in danger because of her.

"Maybe." Rock pocketed the evidence and began walking back down the hill. "Let's get the shell casing turned over to the police. I want to talk to Sergeant Kellen too. He never returned my call last night."

She followed him, her thoughts whirling as they retraced their steps back to town. How had she managed to find that small piece of brass amongst all the leafy debris? It wasn't easy to admit there was a slim possibility Rock was right. That maybe there was a God to counteract the work of the devil, and that He was watching over them. Over her.

A bit late, in her humble opinion. After thirteen years, much of her time with the Preacher was a blur. As if her mind had shut out the worst of what she and her foster siblings had lived through day after day.

The clearest memory she retained was the night of the fire. The choking fear as smoke grew thick in the air. The absolute panic when she thought they'd be trapped down in the cellar to die in the fire.

She couldn't say for sure how they'd gotten out of the cellar. Other than a vague memory that Jayme hadn't been on her blanket when Hailey had sneaked up the stairs only to smell the smoke. She'd gone down and crawled to Sawyer, who'd rousted the rest of the kids. The next thing she knew, they were climbing out of the cellar assisted by Jayme and running into the forest.

The thought that God had planned the fire that had enabled the foster kids to escape seemed ludicrous. Yeah, it was something Rock would say, but she didn't see how something like that was even possible.

Whatever. Her lack of faith wasn't the issue at the moment. The most important thing now was to try to draw this guy out of hiding. Based on the way things were going, she didn't think the Gatlinburg police were going to pick him up anytime soon.

Rock held the door to the police station open for her. The woman behind the desk recognized him, and before he could say anything, she reached for her phone. "Sarg? I have Ranger Wilson here to see you." She listened for a moment, then hung up. "Leave me your weapon and go on in."

Rock already has his gun and holster in his hand. He set them beside her and then headed through the locked door to the cubicle area behind it. Hailey felt herself tense, even though she knew it was silly.

Old habits of avoiding law enforcement were hard to break, even when she hadn't done anything wrong.

"Ranger Wilson," Sergeant Kellen greeted Rock formally. "Ms. Donovan. I assume you're here because of the shooting last night."

"Yeah," Rock drawled. "I left you a message, thanks for getting back to me."

"I'm sorry for the delay," Kellen said with a hint of defensiveness. "I wish I had an update for you, but I don't. I'm sorry, but the cop watching the motel left to respond to a call."

"I heard," Rock said. "And it was likely at that moment, or shortly thereafter, that the shooter took the opportunity to fire at Hailey."

"I know." Kellen suddenly looked exhausted. "This guy is one determined son of a buccaneer; I'll say that much for him."

"I'm here to provide you an update." Rock pulled the bagged shell casing from his pocket. Hailey smiled at the incredulous look on Kellen's face. "Hailey found this up on the hill directly across from the motel. I'd like you to check it for fingerprints, see if you can match it with the partial taken off the knife."

"Ms. Donovan found it?" She bristled at Kellen's skeptical tone.

"Yes, I did." She managed to refrain from adding that she'd found what his officers had missed.

If they'd bothered to look at all.

"I'm impressed, this is great news." Kellen readily took

the bag from Rock. "It's not hunting season, so there's no other reason to have a shell casing lying around. Especially one that looks pretty new. I'll get it right over to the crime lab."

"I'd appreciate that," Rock said. "And please call me as soon as you're able with the results."

"I will." Sergeant Kellen looked flustered. "I really do wish I had better news for you."

"Me too," Hailey said, boldly speaking up. "Considering his guy seems determined to take me out of the picture for good."

Rock put a hand on her arm. "I'm surprised your guys haven't found anyone matching the description of Hailey's sketch yet."

"It's been distributed to every single squad, but you've seen the masses of tourists walking around," Kellen pointed out with a grimace. "Unfortunately, it wouldn't be difficult for this guy to hide in plain sight."

Hailey swallowed her bitter disappointment and turned away. She'd heard enough. By the time she was at the point of leaving the police station, Rock had caught up with her while securing his weapon on his hip.

Out of the corner of her eye, she saw a man seated behind a large sketchbook. She'd noticed people like him before, drawing pictures of tourists for cash.

For a moment she thought he looked familiar, not the assailant, but maybe someone Darby had dated? Before she could edge closer, a phone began to ring.

At first she was confused as it didn't sound like Rock's phone. Then she remembered her disposable one. Only a few people had her number, so she answered with a tentative, "Hello?"

"Hailey? It's Nora. Are you still in Gatlinburg?" Nora sounded breathless, as if she'd been running.

Running herself ragged doing all the work alone, most likely. A flash of guilt hit hard.

"I'm still here," Hailey confirmed. "I want to help you, Nora, but I'm worried about putting you and the customers in danger."

"I know. I won't deny I was pretty steamed when you didn't show up yesterday morning. But after hearing your voice mail, I calmed down and thought about your decision rationally. No one wants to put innocent lives in harm's way, least of all me. But I want to help, are you sure there isn't anything I can do?"

Hailey had to blink back the sting of tears. "The only thing you could do is consider hiring me back after the police manage to catch this guy. I know you need someone now, so I understand if you can't rehire me right away. Just maybe, if the person you bring on board doesn't work out . . ." She let her voice trail off because she knew she was asking a lot.

"Hailey, where do you think I'm going to get help at this late date?" Nora demanded. "All the college kids home for the summer already have jobs. Trust me, I've been asking around, but no one has jumped at the chance to work here. I'll make do without you, but can you try to wrap this up soon? I need you, and not just because of the workload. I miss you. You're one of the closest friends I have."

For a moment, her throat was so tight she couldn't respond. No one had ever needed her before or missed her like Nora claimed. "I'm trying," she said in a choked voice. "Rock Wilson is helping. But there was another attack last night, so I don't dare return to the farm. As much as I'd love nothing more."

"Another gunshot?" Nora sounded horrified. "What in the world is going on?"

"I'm not sure, but the police are working on it," Hailey assured her.

"I'd like to get my hands on the guy doing this to you," Nora said darkly.

"Get in line." She smiled wearily at Rock, who was obviously listening to her side of the conversation. "I think Rock wants first dibs as he's been close to being injured by this guy too."

"I feel so much better knowing Rock is there with you," Nora admitted. "Listen, I have to go. Take care of yourself and get back to work as soon as possible, you hear?"

"I'll do my best," she promised. "Thanks, Nora. For everything." She disconnected from the call and shook her head. "She's being so wonderful about this."

"Told you Nora wouldn't want to lose you," Rock offered a gentle smile. "You have a life here, Hailey. And people who care about you."

"I guess I do." She slid her phone into the front pocket of her jeans. Difficult to believe that just twenty-four hours ago she'd been steely determined to catch a taxi, fleeing to Knoxville. To put as much distance between herself and the shooter as possible.

Now, she wanted more than anything to stay right here in Gatlinburg. She loved her job, the mountains, Nora, and she deeply cared about Rock.

For the first time ever, she found herself envisioning a future that didn't include her living alone in a dumpy trailer but within a community. With friends.

Maybe, even at some point, with Rock.

ROCK HAD BEEN ANNOYED by the lack of progress from the Gatlinburg PD, but his bad mood faded away when he'd overheard Hailey talking to Nora.

He could see by the bemused expression on her face. Hailey hadn't realized how people felt about her. It seemed she was beginning to believe Gatlinburg was her home. And he really wanted to be a part of her life here too. Not just now, keeping her safe from harm, but after this was over.

Previous failed relationships aside, Rock couldn't imagine his life without Hailey. Which didn't make much sense as he'd only known her for a few days.

Yet they'd spent a lot of time together, so much so that he'd learned a lot. Not just her terrible past, but how she functioned under pressure. How she rarely complained, no matter how awful the circumstances were.

Hailey was incredibly independent yet willing to work as a member of the team when needed. Like during the timber rattler incident. She hadn't screamed or become useless. No, she'd gone out to pick up bear scat to use as a snake repellent.

Who else would do such a thing?

No one he knew, that's for sure.

And yeah, he still wanted to fix her, but he was doing his best to give her the room she needed to find her own way. It occurred to him that he could help by simply supporting her, rather than trying to fix her.

They took the trolley over to the mini-golf course, located a bit outside of town. It was difficult to imagine that she'd never once played mini golf. Then again, with a childhood like hers, he shouldn't be surprised. Sad to know she hadn't experienced any of the typical childhood milestones.

Had she even graduated high school? Since it didn't make him think less of her, he wasn't going to ask. But somehow he'd sensed she hadn't. Not by choice but by sheer circumstances alone.

Hadn't she mentioned her priority back then was simply to survive?

He wasn't a violent man by nature, but he was glad to know the Preacher had died in the fire. Even though, death was too good for the guy.

Standing in line to pay for the golf, he braced himself for Hailey's inevitable insistence on paying for herself. To his surprise, she didn't say a word, just took the putter he'd handed her along with a blue golf ball.

She tossed it into the air and caught it. "So how does this work?"

"Are you familiar with golf?"

"Yes, I don't live under a rock," she said dryly.

He grinned. "We count our strokes as we attempt to get the ball in the cup. But each hole has some sort of obstacle in the way that we'll need to maneuver around."

"That doesn't sound too hard," she mused.

"It's not, and besides, it's all for fun." He headed over to the first hole. "Ready?"

"You go first so I can watch how it's done." She leaned on her putter as he placed his ball on the tee. The windmill was spinning slowly, so he did his best to time the shot so that the ball slid beneath unscathed.

Unfortunately, he hit the edge of the paddle as it was going up. The ball spun off to the side and stopped.

"The ball is supposed to go through the opening, right?" Hailey grinned.

"Yeah." He sighed. "Your turn."

Hailey lined up her ball and also tried to gauge when to make her shot. Somehow she managed to miss the windmill, and her ball sailed through the opening to reach the other side.

"Show-off," he muttered as she ran around to see where her ball ended up.

"Rock? I'm only a few inches from the hole, is it okay if I just tap it in?"

He went over to join her, noting her ball was indeed very close to the cup. "Go for it." After she tapped the ball in, he went over to salvage what he could of his game.

Hailey had more trouble on the second hole, where the goal was to get the ball through the clown's narrow mouth. She looked annoyed as their scores tied.

"Competitive, are you?" he teased.

She flushed. "More than I realized."

"Haven't played much in the way of team sports, huh?"

The light went out of her eyes. "No. Too busy trying to survive."

He mentally kicked himself for ruining the mood. "Hey, I never played sports either. Believe it or not, I was more of a science nerd."

She squinted at him. "I guess I can see that. Although I always think of science nerds as having thick glasses."

He grinned and tapped the corner of his eye. "I used to, but I had Lasik surgery after college."

She laughed, and he was relieved she'd shaken off the remnants of the past. "How did you go from science geek to park ranger?"

"Nature is part of science, and I wanted to do something to preserve the wildlife. It wasn't easy, these jobs are highly competitive. I was rejected twice before I finally got in. And that was mainly because the guy ahead of me had gotten himself in trouble with a DUI. If not for his citation,

I may not be here with you right now." And wasn't that a depressing thought?

Or maybe he should look at it from the other side. That God was watching out for him as much as He was watching over Hailey.

"Well, I'm all in favor of preserving wildlife," Hailey said with a nod. "My dream is to save up enough money to buy a small place in the mountains. I'd want to be far away from the tourists here in town. I'd also love a large garden to grow my own veggies."

It was on the tip of his tongue to mention he had a cabin in the mountains with enough land for a garden, but he managed to bite the words back.

One kiss did not make a relationship. Even if all he could think of was kissing her again.

And as much as he wanted to return to his cabin, he wasn't leaving Hailey's side. Not yet.

Not until they had this guy behind bars.

The eighteen-hole mini-golf course took a while to get through. Especially since they weren't in any particular hurry. It was spread out over a large portion of land, and there were a lot of trees to shade them from the relentless sun.

He hoped Hailey was enjoying herself as much as he was. It had been a long time since he'd done something silly just for fun. With a wince, he was forced to admit that this was beginning to feel like a date. As if he'd taken a vacation day. And once this was over, he'd have to deal with his boss's anger, praying the guy wouldn't follow through on his threat to fire him.

Rock was so preoccupied with his thoughts as he tried to get his ball closer to the cup that he didn't see the man creeping out from the brush until it was too late.

"Hailey!" he shouted, knowing he was too far away to prevent the assailant from getting to her.

Hailey turned, lost her footing, and stumbled backward. A man matching Hailey's sketch lunged forward, leading with a large hunting knife.

"NO!" Rock screamed as the knife sliced across Hailey's abdomen. He launched himself at the guy, knocking him off his feet. The assailant grunted when he hit the ground, then went limp. Rock sucked in a breath as he realized the guy had hit his head on the edge of the concrete walkway. Blood pooled from his head wound, and Rock fumbled for his phone to call 911.

"Hey!" Hailey held a hand over the slice across her abdomen as she crawled over to shake the man. "What's your name? Who sent you?"

The man didn't move. Rock quickly explained what had happened to the 911 dispatcher, then turned his attention to Hailey.

"How bad is your wound? Help will be here soon."

"It's not deep." She shook the supine man again. "Who sent you?" Sheer desperation rang from her tone.

Still nothing. As the pool of blood beneath his head grew larger, Rock had a bad feeling that the assailant may not wake up anytime soon.

If ever.

## CHAPTER FIFTEEN

Hailey stared at the man lying on the ground in disbelief, barely feeling the five-inch-long cut he'd inflicted across her stomach. Was he just knocked out? Or was his head injury bad enough that he might not recover?

Leaning close, she frowned as she realized he was older than she'd initially thought. Closer to the midforties.

Who was he? And why did he hate her so much?

She jerked in response to the shriek of sirens responding to Rock's 911 call. Maybe someday she wouldn't associate sirens with her brief stint in juvie.

Maybe.

Rock was going through the guy's pockets. The hunting knife was on the ground where he'd dropped it, her blood staining the blade. There was no sign of the rifle. Would his fingerprints match whatever they found on the shell casing?

Surely there couldn't be two men after her. This guy with the knife had to be the same one who'd been shooting at her.

Right?

"I found his ID," Rock said, opening his wallet. "Does the name Gary Thorne mean anything to you?"

"No. Never heard of him." The cut along her belly was starting to sting. Hailey was grateful it wasn't too bad. If she hadn't fallen backward at Rock's shout, she felt certain she'd be in worse shape.

"Interestingly, the license is from Tennessee, with a Memphis address."

"The other side of the state," she murmured. What had brought him here?

"What's this?" Rock pulled a slip of paper from the man's pocket. A phone number was written on it, with an area code that was not from the Gatlinburg area. He glanced at her. "Do you recognize this number?"

"No. But keep in mind, I didn't use my old disposable phone much prior to it being destroyed."

The only reason she'd purchased the thing at all was because Nora wanted a way to get a hold of her. And Hailey knew it was important to have one while hiking. Even if the mountains had lousy cell service.

"Wait a minute, what are you doing?" She stared as Rock pulled out his phone and dialed the number.

"Listen," he advised, putting the call on speaker.

"Is it done?" a raspy voice asked.

Rock's hazel gaze locked on hers. She shook her head, indicating she didn't recognize the voice.

"Yes," Rock said at the same time the siren wailed even louder.

Silence.

Had they gotten disconnected? Rock quickly pressed a button to call again, but there was no answer. He tried several times, without success. He eventually slid his phone into his pocket. "I'm sure the cops can trace the line."

She nodded, hoping he was right. The words echoed again in her mind.

*Is it done?*

"The caller hired him to kill me," she said in a low voice.

Rock sighed. "Yes, it certainly sounds that way. I should have waited to make the call. I bet the siren scared the guy off."

"Maybe, although if I was dead, there might still be sirens in the background, right?" Had it been a man's voice? Probably, as the timbre had been low and gruff.

Three little words, yet she was no closer to finding out who wanted her dead. She moved back as two paramedics approached with a gurney between them.

"Two injured parties?" the shorter paramedic asked in surprise, eyeing her with concern.

Hailey glanced down at her blood-stained T-shirt. The cut was oozing, but it wasn't that deep. Nothing a few stitches couldn't fix. "He's worse than I am." She waved her hand at Gary Thorne. "He's unconscious from a head injury."

The paramedics knelt beside him to render care, although he did pass over a handful of gauze to place over her own injury. She noticed Rock kept a wary eye on Gary Thorne as if he might jump up at any moment and run away.

A very grim-looking Sergeant Kellen approached. "What happened?"

Rock explained how the man had come out of the brush toward Hailey. "I was behind the crooked schoolhouse on the mini-golf course," he said sourly. "I almost missed seeing him but shouted in time for Hailey to react."

"Rock's shout made me turn so fast, I slipped on the putting green and fell," she said, taking up the story. She lifted a corner of the gauze with a faint grimace. "Thankfully, the knife only scratched me."

"Looks deeper than a scratch," Rock said with a frown. "We need to get you to the hospital."

"I agree," Kellen said.

Rock pinned Kellen with a fierce gaze. "I want Gary Thorne placed under arrest, with a guard on him twenty-four seven. When he wakes up, I want to be there when you question him."

"Demanding, aren't you?" Kellen drawled.

Rock flushed but didn't back down. "This crime started on national parkland. I'm involved and want to see this through."

"Yeah, okay," Kellen agreed with a sigh. "I can see how you'd want to be there through the end of this. I'm sorry Ms. Donovan was hurt, but I'm glad you got him."

"Yeah, but he hasn't said a word about his crimes," Hailey pointed out. "He's a total stranger to me. I have no idea why he wants me dead."

"I found this phone number," Rock said, thrusting the paper at Kellen. "I called and a raspy voice asked, *Is it done?*"

Sergeant Kellen's eyebrows shot up. "Murder for hire?"

Rock nodded. "That's the only explanation I can come up with."

Kellen let out a long, low whistle. "That's interesting."

Interesting? No, it was downright frightening. Because she didn't know anything to cause someone to send a hit man after her. It wasn't as if she'd ever tangled with organized crime or any other sort of criminal enterprise.

The worst thing she'd done was steal money and other goods to feed herself and Darby. That wasn't enough to send someone after her.

Yet if they couldn't figure out who'd hired Gary Thorne, the same person could get another hit man to carry out the same end result. More attempts to kill her.

Her shoulders slumped. They were no further ahead than they were three days ago when this mess had started.

"Hailey? I'm taking you to the hospital." Rock took her arm in a light yet firm grip. "And don't even think about arguing. That cut needs stitches, and I'm not about to risk you getting an infection."

Since the wound had begun to throb, she nodded in agreement. "If Nora didn't fire me, I might even have health insurance."

"Nora hasn't fired you," Rock assured her. He glanced at Kellen. "I need one of your guys to give us a lift to the police station where I left my vehicle. I don't want Hailey to walk that far."

"I can walk, I'm not hurt that badly," she protested. Just the thought of being in the back of a police car made her stomach roll.

"I'll take you, my ride isn't far." Sergeant Kellen spent a few minutes giving instructions to the officers still on scene before leading the way over to the side of the road closest to the seventeenth hole of the mini-golf course.

His vehicle turned out to be a squad car, complete with metal grate separating the people in the back from the driver up front. Rock's hand in the small of her back urged her forward, leaving her little choice but to get inside.

She shivered and hoped her aversion wasn't too obvious. Logically, she knew her reaction was over the top, she wasn't under arrest and was simply being driven to the police station.

But feelings weren't logical.

"Are you okay?" Rock must have picked up on her anxiety. "Is your wound hurting?"

"A little." Better to use that for an excuse.

The trip to the police station didn't take long, and she slid out from the cruiser with a sense of relief. Rock unlocked the SUV and helped her inside.

"Where is the closest hospital?" she asked once they were on the road.

"Not sure. I think LeConte Medical Center is the closest." Rock used his GPS console to pinpoint the location.

"Do you think that's where they took Thorne?"

"Probably. It's less than ten miles from Gatlinburg, heading toward Pigeon Forge."

Hailey wondered again about Darby. Getting a boyfriend to seek revenge on Hailey was one thing, but hiring a hit man? She couldn't fathom that.

She didn't see how or why any of the other foster kids would go to this length either.

Then she thought about the cop in Pigeon Forge who'd wanted sex in exchange for not taking her to jail. It took her a minute to remember his last name, Dayton? No, Doyle. Yes, she'd told her public defender about what he'd said, but her lawyer claimed it was a he-said, she-said scenario that was impossible to prove.

And even though she'd been given a lighter sentence, she'd still ended up in juvie. She'd always thought her lawyer had gotten her sentence knocked down because of her allegation.

But had Doyle gotten into trouble for what he'd tried to do? And even if he had, why on earth would he come after her now? That incident had happened when she'd just turned seventeen. Ten years had passed.

She was so lost in her thoughts she didn't notice when

Rock pulled up in front of the emergency department. Sliding out of the seat, she walked with him inside.

The place looked busy, but it didn't take long for her to be escorted into a room in the back. Rock wanted to come with her, but she made him stay in the waiting room. "I'll be fine," she promised.

Rock hesitated, then said, "I'll give you the privacy you deserve, but if you need me, I'm here for you."

She was touched by his offer. "Thanks."

A resident physician ended up doing her sutures, and the numbing medication hurt far more than the stitches themselves. When she was finished, she casually asked, "Is Gary Thorne still here?"

"I think he's still in the trauma bay," the resident answered. "Why? Do you know him?"

"He's the one who hurt me," she admitted. "I'd like to talk to him, it will only take a minute."

The resident frowned. "I'm afraid that's impossible. The police have him in custody."

"Sergeant Kellen said it was okay." She inwardly winced at the untruth.

"Well, he's still unresponsive and has a breathing tube in place. I'm afraid he's not in any condition to talk to anyone."

She was stunned speechless. A breathing tube didn't sound good.

What if Thorne never regained consciousness?

Would she have to give up her life in Gatlinburg after all?

ROCK JUMPED up when Hailey crossed over to him. "Hey, you okay?"

"Fine." Her smile didn't reach her eyes. "I have to take antibiotics, keep the sutures dry, and have them removed in ten days." She held up a small bag. "They already gave me the antibiotics."

"Great." He escorted her to the door. "Hailey, Sergeant Kellen told me Thorne's fingerprints match the knife found at the bus station and a partial print on the shell casing. He's the guy responsible for everything that's happened to you." He hesitated, then added, "He's not doing well from what I hear. But I still think it's safe enough for you to go home."

"Home?" Hope flared in her eyes. Then she shook her head. "No, I can't do that. We don't know who hired him."

"True, but do you really think the person on the other end of the phone is going to stick around? Whoever he is, he has to suspect the police will be trying to find him by tracing the number."

Hailey shrugged, looking unconvinced. "Even if I'm safe now, how long do you think that will last?"

"I don't know," Rock admitted. "We may learn more over the next few days as the police track Thorne's whereabouts. They'll figure out where he was staying, what type of car he's driving, even the rifle he'd used. Hopefully, they'll uncover another clue as to who hired him."

Hailey was silent as she slid into the passenger seat of his SUV. When he was settled behind the wheel, she reached over to touch his arm. "Rock, I think I need to tell the police a few things."

His heart soared. Did she finally trust him enough to tell him what she knew? "What sort of things? About the foster kids you lived with?"

She dropped her hand and looked away. "That, and an

incident that occurred a long time ago. It's hard to imagine that he's holding a grudge all this time, but I think Sergeant Kellen should know."

"Okay," he agreed slowly. "I'll give him a call to make sure he has time to talk."

"Good." The way she twisted her fingers in her lap betrayed the extent of her nervousness.

Rock wished he could assure her that there was nothing she could say to make him think any less of her. If that's what she was worried about.

He called the police station and was instantly put through to Kellen. "I don't have anything new to tell you, Wilson," he said in an annoyed tone. "I told you I'd let you know when I did."

"That's not why I'm calling. Ms. Donovan has some information to share with you. If you have time," he added hastily.

Kellen sighed loudly. "Yeah, okay, although it would have been nice if she'd come forward sooner. I guess I can talk to her."

"I'd appreciate that," Rock said, understanding the sergeant's frustration.

"I have Detective Larson working the case," Kellen continued. "I pulled him off from his vacation time, we generally don't have a lot of high-level crime here, so we only have one detective on staff. The good news is that Larson has already found the motel where Thorne was staying. It wasn't very far from yours."

"Great work," Rock praised, although hearing the guy had been staying nearby was an unwelcome surprise. "We're still at the hospital, so it'll take us roughly twenty minutes to get there."

"That's fine, see you soon." Kellen disconnected from

the call.

Rock set his phone in the console between the seats and started the engine. Hailey still looked apprehensive, yet she didn't indicate she'd changed her mind as he drove out of the hospital parking lot.

"It's going to be okay," he said, breaking the prolonged silence.

"Is it?" Hailey grimaced. "I wish I could be so sure."

He knew he had to tread carefully. "I know you don't believe in God, but I do. And I know God is watching over you. He's kept you safe so far."

"Sort of," she agreed. She placed her hand gingerly over her abdomen. He could see white gauze through the slice in her bloody T-shirt, and he belatedly realized he should have taken the time to buy a replacement for her.

After their meeting with Sergeant Kellen, he silently promised. He'd buy her new clothes and feed her before taking her home.

By the time he pulled up to the police station, Hailey's fingers were twisted together again. He felt bad she was so stressed about this upcoming discussion. Hopefully, once she'd told the police everything she knew, baring secrets long held and deeply buried, she'd feel better.

He was a firm believer that confession was good for the soul.

"Let's get this over with," she muttered as she shoved open her door.

Rock walked her inside, hesitating before approaching the desk. "Hailey, I want to be there for you, to support you through this ordeal. But I don't want to make things worse either." It cost him a lot to add, "If you'd rather talk to Kellen alone, I'll understand."

To his surprise, she reached out and grasped his hand.

"I'd rather you stay with me." Her smile was lopsided. "You know more about my past than anyone. I hardly think this small bit of additional information will shock you."

He squeezed her hand and wished he could pull her into his arms for a hug and a kiss. "Thanks for trusting me," he managed. "I'm happy to stay with you."

Hailey nodded and moved toward the front desk. Rock listened as the woman told Kellen they were here and went through the process of securing his weapon.

Sergeant Kellen was waiting for them outside the interview room. He looked wary, as if unsure of what to expect from Hailey. "Ms. Donovan," he greeted her with a nod.

"Sergeant." Hailey headed inside the room. "I don't want to waste your time, but I did think of something while I was at the hospital that I think you should know."

"Talking to victims is never a waste of time," Kellen said, taking the seat across from her. "Any information can be helpful in this kind of investigation."

She stared down at her interlaced fingers for a long moment. "I'm sure you're aware of my juvenile record," she said quietly.

Kellen briefly met Rock's gaze, then nodded. "Yes, however, your record is sealed." He frowned. "You think Gary Thorne is part of what happened back then?"

"I don't, not really. I was stealing jewelry," she began, talking fast. "I was hungry and so was my foster sister, Darby. We hadn't eaten in days, and the tourist season had ended, so pickings were scarce." Hailey continued looking down at her lap. "I got greedy, thought that if I took enough jewelry, it would last us a while, rather than having to go out looking for more to steal every couple of days. I was tired of not knowing when our next meal would be as we bounced from shelter to shelter."

Rock noticed Kellen wasn't taking notes, and he thought he saw a glimmer of compassion in his dark eyes.

"Of course, I got caught." Rock noticed her fingers tightened until her knuckles were white. "The Pigeon Forge cop who arrested me was a man named Doyle. He told me I could either have sex with him or he'd arrest me and throw me in jail."

Rock went still, unable to breathe. He wanted to punch something, or someone, specifically Doyle, but of course that wasn't an option.

"I chose jail," Hailey went on. "I told my public defender about what Doyle had done, but it was my word against his, and I was a thief, right? He told me no one would listen. The DA's office wanted to charge me as an adult with a felony crime because of the high value of the jewelry in my possession. I think my lawyer must have said something about the sex bargain because I was only charged with a misdemeanor and as a juvenile instead of an adult."

There was a long silence before Kellen spoke. "I'm very sorry to hear you had to go through that, Ms. Donovan."

She shrugged. "It wasn't your fault. I only brought it up because Doyle could be holding a grudge if my allegation caused him problems down the road. Although I don't see how they could have had any impact, at least according to my lawyer."

Rock balled his hands into fists. As if it wasn't bad enough, Hailey was struggling to survive, but to be asked for sex by a cop whose job it was to uphold the law?

He didn't blame her for not trusting the police. And her confession only made him admire her more.

Admire? No, his feelings were far stronger than that. She wouldn't want to hear it, but he was falling in love with her.

# CHAPTER SIXTEEN

It hadn't been easy to dredge up the horrible memories of the past, but Hailey was surprisingly relieved once the entire ugly story was out in the open. Her body felt light, as if freed of a heavy burden.

She was relieved that Sergeant Kellen actually believed her. And really, as long as she'd come this far, she may as well keep going. "There's one more thing," she said, breaking the silence.

"More?" Rock asked in a hoarse voice.

She risked a glance at him, frowning at his pale face and tense muscles. "I explained to you about the Preacher, but Sergeant Kellen doesn't know."

"Oh, yes. Of course." He looked chagrined.

She briefly explained about the Preacher's physical abuse, how he'd made them sleep in the cellar, the fire, and their ultimate escape. She glossed over the awful details but could tell Kellen understood how bad it had been.

"There were seven of us foster kids, and we all split up after we escaped. Darby and I ended up in Pigeon Forge. Darby is only two years younger than me, so she's twenty-five by now. Darby had gotten mixed up in a rough crowd; her boyfriend, Aaron, was a small-time drug dealer and verbally abusive. We had a huge fight about her relationship with Aaron. I told her the reason I wanted to get the jewelry was so that we could move to a new place, far from Aaron and his friends. She screamed at me, claiming she hated me and loved Aaron. Then she left. After I was released from my stint in juvie, she and Aaron were gone."

"Do you know Aaron's last name?" Kellen asked.

"No, and I haven't been able to find Darby either. At first, I thought she'd come after me, maybe because something bad happened to Aaron." She avoided Rock's gaze. "After all, the attacks were personal, and Darby was the only one who was furious with me and knew me on a personal level. But now, I'm not so sure. The voice on the phone didn't sound anything like Darby." She fell silent, somewhat relieved to dump all this in his lap, to let him decide what to do.

Especially if there was any chance that he'd find Darby.

Kellen scratched a few notes on his pad. "What are the names of the other foster kids?"

"Sawyer Murphy is my age, we were close at the time. He's a cop in Chattanooga, so I think you can take him off your list," she added wryly. "Cooper, Trent, and Sawyer all went off on their own, but I don't know what Cooper's and Trent's last names are. I spoke to Sawyer yesterday, he didn't seem to know where they were either. Jayme was the oldest, and she took the youngest girl, Caitlin, with her. Caitlin was only nine back when we escaped, and I'd hoped one day to meet up with Jayme and Caitlin, but I never did. I don't know where they ended up."

"And the Preacher?" Kellen asked.

"He and his wife, Ruth, died in the fire. We all scouted

the woods surrounding the cabin, without finding the Preacher or his wife anywhere."

"So why did you run away?" Kellen asked.

"We were still minors, and we all agreed we'd never go back into the foster system." Hailey lifted her chin. "Do you blame us?"

"No, I can't blame you," Kellen agreed.

There. That was everything. She sat back in her chair, feeling weak. She hadn't wanted to implicate any of the fosters, but hearing those raspy words coldly asking, *Is it done?* made her realize that if Darby or any of the others had hired Thorne to kill her, then they weren't the same kids she remembered.

People changed. And dire circumstances often made people change in a bad way. Hadn't she come close to giving up more than once? Desperation could drive a person to do something drastic.

Although hiring a hit man, and a rather inept one at that, seemed over the top. But she supposed anything was possible.

If Darby needed help, she'd do her best to provide that for her. But Hailey also knew it might be too late. Darby may be too far gone, or even—*dead.*

She didn't want to consider her younger sister might have died. But so far her attempts to find Darby had been futile. Clearly, Darby hadn't tried to find her.

The knowledge stung and only added to the possibility that Darby was still angry with her.

Rock's arm dropped around her shoulders in a comforting embrace. After a moment's hesitation, she leaned against him, drawing on his strength.

"You've been through a lot, Ms. Donovan," Kellen said in a low voice. "I know it wasn't easy for you to tell me all this, but I want to thank you for coming in today. These are possibilities we'll be happy to investigate." He scowled. "Especially Doyle."

"Sure." She nodded and straightened, pulling away from Rock. "I'm sorry I didn't tell you everything sooner. But I honestly didn't think that anything that happened ten years ago could be relevant now."

"Ten years is a long time, but I've seen plenty of circumstances where people can't let go of an old grudge." Kellen stood, so she pushed to her feet as well. "Thanks again, Ms. Donovan."

She nodded and turned toward the door.

"Please keep me updated on the progress of your investigation," Rock said to Kellen, before joining her in the hall.

"I'm glad that's over," she said as they returned to the front desk.

"I can imagine." Rock took his weapon from the lockbox and secured it to his belt. "Let's get out of here."

Hailey paused to glance around the interior of the police station. Oddly enough, it didn't seem nearly as intimidating as it had during her first visit.

Maybe coming inside so many times had made her immune to the impact. That and knowing that Sergeant Kellen and the other cops here, other than Morrison, would never treat her the way Doyle had.

Even Morrison, jerk that he'd been, hadn't made any advances on her. Although he might have if Rock hadn't been standing there in his uniform. Either way, Morrison wasn't going to be a problem. She wasn't a scared kid anymore.

She headed outside, realizing her stomach was rumbling. The resident had told her it would be best to take her antibiotic with meals.

"Hailey." Rock's soft voice made her turn to face him.

"Yes?"

"I need a hug."

She thought she'd misheard him, but then he drew her into his arms and held her close. She wrapped her arms around his waist and hugged him back.

"Me too," she whispered against his chest.

He held her for a long time, seemingly unwilling to let her go. Finally, still holding her, he leaned back just far enough to look down into her eyes. "I want to punch Doyle for what he did to you," Rock confessed in a low voice. "If he is responsible for hiring Thorne, I hope and pray he rots in jail for the rest of his life."

"I hope so too." She couldn't deny she'd secretly fantasized about punching Doyle herself. "But that was a long time ago. Aaron is another possibility."

"You are such an incredible woman," he murmured.

She blushed and lowered her gaze to stare at the button of his uniform shirt. "I just did what was necessary to survive."

"Hailey." His low, rough tone made her shiver with awareness. "I'd like to kiss you."

Her blush deepened. Never in her life had any man asked to kiss her. It felt awkward yet special at the same time. She lifted her gaze to his. "Okay."

He chuckled, then captured her mouth with his. There was no hesitancy in his kiss, and she reveled in the possessive yet sweet sensation.

Finally, he broke off the kiss, gulping deep breaths. "I think we have an audience."

"Huh?" She had no idea what he meant until she noticed several tourists gawking at them. She hid her face against his chest. "Good grief."

He laughed. "I don't mind, but I figured you might. Come on, I think it's time I feed you. Your stomach was rumbling the entire time we were kissing."

"I have a high metabolism," she said defensively.

"I don't mind." He grinned. "I like feeding you. And no, we're not having fast food again. We're going to the Starlight Inn. Consider this our first date."

"Date?" she echoed in a squeaky voice.

"Yes, date. After we eat, I'm going to buy you a new T-shirt and then take you home. We're going to fix up your trailer, then let Nora know you'll be back to work tomorrow."

His plan sounded good; in fact, it was exactly what she wanted, but she instinctively dug in her heels. "One kiss doesn't mean you can make decisions for me."

He stopped and looked at her with a puzzled frown. "That's not what I'm doing."

"Yes, it is." She swallowed hard but decided she needed to stand up for herself. "You could ask me to lunch. You could ask me if I want to shop for a new shirt, which I don't. I still have several in my backpack. You could ask me if I'm ready to go home and back to work."

He nodded, looking apologetic. "Okay, point taken. Hailey, would you please have lunch with me?"

She hesitated, sensing this was a turning point in their relationship. More so than their incredibly sensual kiss, which she wanted very badly to experience again. "Yes, Rock, I'll have lunch with you."

"Thank you." Rock took her hand in his. "Be patient with me, I haven't been in a relationship for a long time."

Really? "Speaking of which, why not? A guy like you should have a girlfriend."

Rock hesitated, then said, "Apparently, I'm bossy and work too much."

She laughed, then winced and put a hand over her injury. "That's exactly what Jacob said to me, before he mentioned he'd found someone new."

"That means we're perfect for each other," Rock said with a wide smile.

Hailey wasn't sure she'd go that far, but for now, going on a date with Rock was a nice place to start.

Even though she'd never rest easy until the person who'd hired Gary Thorne was in police custody.

ROCK KNEW he'd almost blown things with Hailey and did his best to make amends. As frustrating as it was, he didn't press the shopping expedition, but he did ask that she let him help her clean up the mess in her trailer.

"Don't you have a job to worry about?" she asked in an exasperated tone. "I'd rather you make amends with your boss."

"I can do that tomorrow, the day's already half over."

She peered at him over the rim of her iced tea. "Are you a procrastinator?"

"No." He blew out a breath, hating to admit she was right. The sooner he talked to his boss, the better. "Fine. Have it your way."

"I will."

They left the Starlight Inn and climbed into his SUV. His phone rang, and Sergeant Kellen's name flashed on the screen. "Wilson," he answered.

"Rock, is Ms. Donovan with you?" Kellen asked.

"Yes." He glanced at Hailey who was listening intently. "What's up?"

"I'm sorry to tell you both that Gary Thorne just died without regaining consciousness."

Rock sighed. "I'm sorry to hear that."

"Me too. Doesn't mean we won't find out who hired him, but it might take longer than we'd hoped. We're still going through his information, looks as if he was paid five thousand dollars five days ago. Unfortunately, he deposited cash into his account, so there's no way to trace it."

Rock felt his hopes plummet. The chances of finding out who hired the guy were dwindling fast. "Thanks for the update."

"The other thing we learned is that the phone number you called is from Memphis."

"Same place as Thorne lived?" Rock asked.

"Yes, although that only means that's where the phone was purchased. Sorry I don't have better news."

"I understand." Rock disconnected from the line.

"I'm not really safe, am I?" Hailey asked softly.

"You're safe from Thorne, but I can't deny there's a slim possibility that the person who hired him could try again."

"Slim possibility?" She let out a harsh laugh. "I think it's more of a high probability that he'll eventually try again."

"I don't," Rock argued. "Especially since I specifically told the person the job was done. It could be that he never planned to pay Thorne the rest of his money and that's why he hung up so abruptly. The sirens might not have had anything to do with ending the call."

"That's a lot of mights and maybes," Hailey said glumly.

True, but what else could he say? He didn't want her to move away, didn't want her to start over someplace new.

The ride out of town to the Whispering Oaks Trailer

Park didn't take long. He pulled up in the small parking space and quickly hopped out.

He wanted to be sure there was no one lurking around inside.

Hailey pulled her backpack out of the rear seat and joined him.

"Please let me go in first," he said. "Just in case."

With reluctance, she stepped back. Entering the trailer, he swept a glance around, taking note that the place looked no different than the last time he'd been there. Moving quickly, he went from room to room to make sure no one was hiding inside.

"It's clear." He turned to see Hailey standing in the doorway, a terrified look on her face. And a large obese man holding a gun pressed into her side.

"Put your weapon down, nice and slow," the big man said in a low gruff tone.

Doyle. This guy had to be the cop that had wanted sex in exchange for not arresting Hailey. And he recognized the voice on the phone asking, *Is it done?* "Doyle, right? The Gatlinburg police are looking for you."

The statement seemed to surprise him, but Doyle didn't loosen his grip. "The weapon. She'll die if you try anything. My life is worthless anyway, but it'll be a toss-up as to which one of us is still standing when this is over."

Rock held Doyle's gaze, feeling sick at the turn of events. He should have kept Hailey close at his side. Because of his lapse in judgment, Doyle had her at gunpoint. "Okay, cool your jets, I'll put down my weapon."

Doyle pushed Hailey forward into the trailer. Rock carefully reached for his weapon and slowly pulled it from the holster.

There had to be a way out of this situation, but he didn't

want to jolt Doyle into doing something rash. He met Hailey's gaze, and she gave a tiny nod, then sharply elbowed Doyle in his large gut, and at the same time she stomped hard on his foot and threw her head back to smack him in the face.

Caught off guard, Doyle staggered backward. The minute the gun wasn't pressed against Hailey, Rock fired at him.

Hailey dropped and rolled away from Doyle, coming up to stand on her feet. Doyle was slumped against the doorway of the trailer, his left hand pressing against the hollow between his chest and his shoulder, his right hand holding the gun down at his side.

"Put the gun down," Rock said sharply. "Now!"

Doyle's face was pale, and beads of sweat formed on his brow. His right hand released the gun, and it fell soundlessly to the floor.

Before Rock could say anything, Hailey rushed forward, scooped up the gun by the barrel, and backed away. "It was you, wasn't it?" she accused. "You hired Thorne to kill me. And when that didn't work, you decided to finish the job yourself."

"You ruined my career. They did an investigation, and others came forward . . ." Doyle's voice grew faint. "It was all your fault . . ."

Others? Rock handed Hailey his phone. "Call 911, then let Sergeant Kellen know we have Doyle."

Hailey took the phone and made the calls. Rock kept his gaze on Doyle, who looked as if he might pass out at any moment.

"Help me," Doyle pleaded. "Don't let me die."

"Help you the way you helped Hailey back when she was stealing to feed herself and her foster sister? That kind of help?" Rock knew he was being unreasonable and quickly approached Doyle. The big man was losing a lot of blood, but he didn't think the bullet had hit his heart. "Hailey, get me some towels."

Hailey fetched the ripped towels from the tiny bathroom as she spoke to Kellen. "Yes, Sergeant. He's here and held me at gunpoint. I fought back, and Rock shot him."

Rock pressed the towels against the wound in Doyle's upper chest with his left hand while holding the gun pressed against the man with his right. The former cop looked too weak to try anything, but he wasn't taking any chances.

Not with Hailey's life.

## CHAPTER SEVENTEEN

Hailey couldn't seem to stop shaking, although she did her best to hide the impact of being held at gunpoint. Even those days with the Preacher paled in comparison to knowing that if Doyle pulled the trigger, she'd be dead.

*Dead.*

For a moment, she glanced upward, wondering once again if God was indeed watching over them.

Watching over her.

There was no denying that escaping Doyle had been something of a miracle. And maybe, just maybe, Rock was right about good versus evil.

*Thank you, God.*

"Hailey?" Rock's expression was grim as he pressed the towels against Doyle's wound. "Are you sure you're not hurt?"

"I'm fine." She knelt beside him. "I'm more concerned about you."

Rock grimaced. "I've never shot a man before. Yet, under the exact same circumstances, I'd do it again."

Guilt pummeled her. "I'm sorry. I shouldn't have let him grab me."

"What?" Rock looked surprised, then shook his head. "No, this isn't your fault. I should have done a better job of protecting you." He hesitated, then said, "Check for a pulse, would you?"

She did as he asked, feeling the faint beat of his heart. "He still has a pulse, but it's weak."

"Good. I want him to rot in jail," Rock said.

She stared at the unconscious Doyle for a long moment. "I can't believe that after all these years, he hired Thorne to kill me."

"Don't dwell on it, Hailey." Rock's brow furrowed with concern. Here he was, trying to reassure her, when he was the one forced to shoot a man for the very first time in his life. All because of her.

And what if Doyle died? How would Rock feel then?

"Hailey?" Rock's deep voice dragged her gaze to his. "Don't take this on yourself. Doyle is responsible for what happened here today, not you."

Logically, she knew Rock was right. What had Doyle said? She'd ruined his life? There were others? What about the lives he'd ruined? The girls he'd forced to have sex in order to avoid going to jail? Because she felt certain she hadn't been the first, or the last. Especially the way he'd mentioned how others had come forward.

A surge of anger hit hard, but she managed to wrestle it under control. There was nothing more she could do to Doyle now. If he survived his injuries, he'd go to jail where he belonged.

He'd never have the opportunity to hurt another young girl ever again.

The sound of sirens split the air. She rose and walked outside to show the EMTs in.

Of course, the ambulance wasn't alone, two squads pulled up alongside as well. She recognized Officer Perkins from when he responded to the gunfire at the motel. And, of course, Sergeant Kellen was there too.

"What happened?" Kellen demanded as Perkins and the two EMTs rushed inside.

Hailey briefly explained again how Rock had gone inside the trailer to make sure it was safe and Doyle had snuck up behind her and pressed his gun against her side. She described how she'd used self-defense to escaped long enough for Rock to shoot Doyle.

Kellen's expression turned grim. "How's Doyle doing?"

"He has a pulse, but it's weak." Hailey hesitated, then asked, "I hope Rock doesn't get into trouble over this. Doyle made it clear he was going to kill us both."

Kellen blew out a deep breath. "It sounds like a case of self-defense, but we still need to investigate. Especially if Doyle doesn't make it."

It wasn't what she wanted to hear, yet she also understood the law. If Doyle died, Rock could be charged with a crime, unless the investigation proved he'd fired in self-defense.

Yet she and Rock were the only witnesses to what happened. And she had a juvie criminal record.

Would anyone believe her?

A spurt of fear hit hard. What if Rock suffered because of her? Putting his job on the line had been bad enough, but this could end badly.

She sent up a silent prayer that Rock would be found innocent of any wrongdoing. She quickly followed Sergeant Kellen inside the trailer. The small space shrank exponentially with the number of people stuffed inside the cramped interior.

It didn't take long for the EMTs to bundle Doyle onto the gurney and rush him out to the ambulance. Hailey sensed time was of the essence, and her spirits sank even further.

"Rock? I need a few moments of your time," Kellen said after Rock washed Doyle's blood from his hands. "Alone."

Rock glanced at her for a moment, then looked away and nodded. "Of course."

Hailey swallowed hard and paced the interior of her small trailer. When she began to clean up the mess Doyle or Thorne had made, Officer Perkins stopped her.

"Sorry, ma'am, but this is a crime scene. I need you to leave everything as it is."

Resigned, she nodded. Moments later, Rock returned with Kellen. "Everything okay?" She looked from Rock's face to Kellen's, trying to read their bland expressions.

"I think I have what I need," Kellen said.

"Glad to hear it," Rock said mildly.

"Wait a minute, what does that mean?" she asked in frustration. "Is Rock in trouble for shooting Doyle or not?"

"Not." Kellen offered a lopsided smile. "I firmly believe this was self-defense, and that's what I'm putting in my report."

"Thank goodness," Hailey whispered.

"Tell her the rest," Rock suggested. "As one of his victims, she deserves to know."

Kellen shrugged and nodded. "I began digging into Doyle as a suspect the minute you left my office. I discovered Doyle spent time in jail after several other allegations similar to yours came forward. It took a while, but someone finally noticed."

"How?" Hailey was intrigued at the news.

"Apparently, they performed a little sting operation with an undercover cop who looked far younger than her actual age. She wore a wire and caught Doyle's bribe on the record. Doyle was sent to jail and just got out a few weeks ago."

Hailey felt her jaw drop. "He was busted by an undercover cop?" Wasn't that some sort of poetic justice.

"That's correct." Kellen glanced at her ruined trailer. "I'm sorry you had to go through all this, Hailey. Sounds like Doyle really had it in for you. According to his cellmate, he constantly railed against you. Because you refused him and got him tossed in jail."

"He must have been obsessed," Rock said grimly. "Now you need to find a connection between Doyle and Thorne to put the case to rest once and for all."

"We will," Kellen said confidently. He hesitated, then added, "I want you both to know I've convinced Morrison to take early retirement. He has his twenty-five years in, so he accepted my deal. Well, that and because his choice was to retire or be fired. One complaint was bad enough, but this last one pushed me over the edge."

"Retirement is almost too good for him," Rock said with a hint of bitterness.

"Yeah, well, some of that is on me. I should have been more in tune as to what he was doing. Or rather not doing." Kellen sighed and looked at the messy trailer again. "Again, please accept my sincere apology, Hailey."

"It's okay." She forced a smile. "I'll be honest, I feel better knowing Doyle is in custody. And that Morrison won't be a cop anymore."

"Good." Kellen glanced at Rock. "That's all I need for now, but I may have more questions down the road."

"We're not going anywhere," Rock assured him. It was a measure of how far she'd come that she didn't resent Rock for including her in that statement.

In fact, now that this was over, she'd miss spending time with him. Being with him.

Kissing him.

She froze as realization dawned.

How on earth had she fallen in love with Rock Wilson?

ROCK WAS RELIEVED Sergeant Kellen had deemed his shooting Doyle as self-defense. He'd never in his life shot a man before and sincerely hoped to never be in a situation where he had to do it again.

Watching Doyle fade in front of his eyes had been difficult. He'd silently prayed Doyle would survive his injury. And if Doyle didn't survive, he'd have to find some solace in knowing he'd shot the man because it was either hit Doyle or lose Hailey.

An easy choice. One he'd make again without the slightest hesitation.

God had been watching over them big time.

"Thanks," Hailey said, looking at Sergeant Kellen. "I appreciate everything you did for both of us."

Kellen nodded and headed toward the door. Then abruptly paused and glanced back over his shoulder. "Rock, I noticed your degree is in criminal justice. If you ever decide to give up being a park ranger, there's always a job waiting for you within the Gatlinburg PD. If you're interested, that is."

Really? "Thanks, I appreciate that," Rock said.

Kellen turned and left, leaving Officer Perkins to man

the crime scene. Rock hoped he wouldn't have to take the sergeant up on his offer. But it was nice to have a backup plan in case his boss gave him the boot.

"I'm sorry, but I need to ask both of you to leave the trailer," Officer Perkins said. "The crime scene techs will be here any minute." The officer paused, then added, "Oh, and I just got word over the radio that Doyle was taken into surgery. Looks like he might make it."

"Thanks for the update." He couldn't deny being slightly relieved the guy would survive. It was fitting that he'd spend the rest of his sorry life in jail.

He followed Hailey outside. She hesitated, then went back toward the trailer doorway to pick up her backpack.

"I dropped it when Doyle caught me off guard," she said sheepishly. "I should have kept it, maybe I could have used it as a weapon."

"You did fine with your elbow, foot, and head butt," Rock said with admiration. "When you locked eyes with me, I lost ten years off my life knowing you were about to do something drastic."

"I wanted to get far enough away so you could shoot," she admitted. Her expression turned grim. "Thank you, Rock. For saving my life."

"Any time," he said, meaning it. Then he frowned. "Are you sure you're okay?"

"Yes, because it's finally over. I was beginning to lose hope I'd ever be safe again." Then she shot a woeful glance at her trailer. "Looks like they'll be in there for a while. Guess I'll be camping beneath the stars tonight."

Not if he had anything to say about it. Still, he hesitated, not sure she was ready.

Deep down, he knew neither one of them should be

alone tonight. Not after what had happened here today. First the near miss at the mini-golf course, now this.

Rock stepped closer to Hailey, took both of her hands in his, and brought them up to his chest, pressing them firmly over his heart. "Hailey, will you please stay with me at my cabin?"

"I'm not living with you, Rock." Her tone was firm. "Thanks for the offer, but no."

"It wouldn't be like that," he protested. "No strings, Hailey. You should know by now I'd never take advantage of you. I want you to be comfortable."

"I've camped out plenty of times," she said with a shrug.

He swallowed a flash of impatience. "But it's not necessary. Not after all this." He could tell she wasn't about to change her mind and blew out a frustrated breath. "Don't you understand? I love you."

She blinked, frowned, and said, "What?"

"I love you, Hailey Donovan. And I know it's too soon for you, and that we barely know each other, but that doesn't change how I feel."

"Rock, you don't know everything about me," she began.

"I know enough," he insisted, cutting her off. "I know you're strong, independent, hardworking, successful, and determined."

"You forgot obstinate and uneducated," she said with a troubled frown.

"You're smart, Hailey. Education doesn't just come from the classroom. And I find your stubbornness cute, most of the time." He hesitated, then added, "I know you don't believe in God, but I'll accept you for who you are, not who I'd like you to be. I love you. Please give me a chance to show you how much."

Her clear blue eyes clung to his for so long he began to

lose hope. Then she cleared her throat. "Yeah, about that. I think you were right about good offsetting evil."

His heart soared. "What makes you think so?"

"Because you, Nora, Sergeant Kellen, and even Officer Perkins are all proof there's good in the world." She hesitated, then added, "I think God must exist or the devil would have taken over the entire world by now."

He lowered his head, pressing a kiss to their clasped hands. "I know God is watching over us. The problem is that some people choose to follow the devil, like your Preacher."

"And Doyle," she added. "I felt certain that God was guiding me as I used self-defense to escape him."

"Doyle and Thorne too. Which is exactly my point. People choose every day, Hailey. We choose to follow and become evil or we choose love and to follow God. It makes me very happy to know you've chosen to follow God."

"Believing in God is one thing, but I'm not ready to attend church," she warned softly. "Especially if the preaching is centered on how we'll go to hell if we don't follow God's word. I've already been in hell, and I'd rather not hear about it."

"I will never pressure you into attending church, Hailey." Although it pained him a bit to think she couldn't find solace there the way he had. "God understands your heart and your mind. We can pray in the woods, which is where I tend to do a lot of my worshiping."

She nodded, and he tried not to be depressed that she hadn't said the words back to him. After all, he was the one rushing things along.

He should be grateful she'd at least opened herself up to faith and God. It was more than he'd ever expected.

He was so proud of how far she'd come.

"Hailey, will you consider spending some time at my cabin while I talk to my boss? We can't clean your place up until they release it as a crime scene."

Hailey glanced around the trailer. "And when will that be?"

"I don't know, but I doubt it will be before tomorrow." He felt bad for her. The small slice of home she'd managed to create had been brutally damaged.

It made him glad to know Doyle could never hurt her again.

"Don't camp out, Hailey," he said in a low voice. "If you do, I'll feel compelled to make camp beside you, to watch over you. Which means both of us will have a lousy night."

"You would, huh?" A smile tipped the corner of her mouth.

"Yes, although it would be a waste of two perfectly comfortable beds. In two separate bedrooms," he stressed.

"Okay."

He hesitated, wondering if he'd missed something. "Okay, what?"

Her smile widened. "Yes, Rock, I'll come stay at your cabin until we can get my place livable."

"Thank you." He pressed a kiss to her hands, then forced himself to take a step back. Cleaning the trailer would take time and energy, but if that's what she wanted, he'd be happy to help.

"I'm grateful, Hailey. You've made my day by agreeing to come with me. Bring your backpack, you can use the shower at my place while I talk to my boss." And pray he still had a job. He rubbed the back of his neck while heading toward his SUV. Maybe once his boss heard everything, he'd let him off with a simple disciplinary action.

"Rock?"

He turned to look at her. "Yeah?"

"I love you too."

He froze, hoping he hadn't imagined it. "You do?"

A smile bloomed on her face. "Yes, I do. It's sweet you don't want to rush me, but I've known since our first kiss how much I care about you."

She had kissed him first. A goofy grin formed on his face. "I'm glad to hear my feelings aren't one-sided."

"They aren't. There is one thing, though." Her expression turned serious.

"Anything," he said, knowing he'd do whatever necessary to make her happy.

"Sometime soon I want to visit Sawyer in Chattanooga. And I want to see if he'll help us find the rest of my foster siblings. It's important to me, and something I should have tried harder to accomplish sooner."

He nodded and gathered her into his arms. "I'm totally on board with that plan. I just hope they're doing as well as you and Sawyer are."

"Me too." Her smile was sad. "But I don't care if they're not, I just want to find them and offer to help with whatever they need."

Her generosity was humbling. "Of course. Anything important to you is equally important to me. I want to make you happy, Hailey."

"You have." Her smile brightened. "Despite being in constant danger, I've been very happy spending these past few days with you. And honestly, I was sad to know our time together was coming to an end."

"I love you so much." He pulled her in for another deep kiss.

"I love you too," she whispered when they had to

breathe. "Let's get out of here. I'm curious to see what kind of place you live in."

"Uh-oh," he groaned as they walked arm in arm toward his SUV. "It's probably not as clean as it could be."

"You're worried about how clean it is? After what we just left behind?" Hailey laughed, the musical sound lifting his spirits. "As long as you don't expect me clean up after you, I think we'll be fine."

He reached over to take her hand. "There's give and take in every relationship, Hailey, and I promise to do my share in this arrangement. I won't take advantage of you. We'll take things slow and easy. I'll happily wait as long as you need."

"Being with you is fast and new for me, but it feels right." She squeezed his hand in return and flashed a grin. "And I promise I won't take advantage of you either."

That made him chuckle. He'd already given her his heart and didn't regret it for a single moment. "I'm not worried. We make a great team."

"We do," Hailey agreed. She reached over and rested her hand on his arm.

Reveling in the warmth of her touch, Rock drove down the highway in the dazzling sunshine toward his rustic cabin. He'd never felt more content and in love as he did at that moment, and he silently thanked God for bringing Hailey into his life.

He vowed to do whatever was necessary to make her happy. Which meant finding the rest of her foster siblings very soon. And with God guiding them, he was sure they would succeed.


READY TO READ Sawyer and Naomi's story? Click here!

# DEAR READER

Welcome to my Smoky Mountain Secrets series! I hope you enjoyed *Hailey's Haven* and are looking forward to reading about Sawyer and Naomi in *Sawyer's Secret*. The rest of the books in order are, *Darby's Decision, Cooper's Choice, Trent's Trust,* and *Jayme's Journey*. I wanted to write a story showcasing the power of God's love and how even those who'd experienced the worst can find their way back to God's loving arms.

Reviews are very important to authors, so if you liked this story, please consider leaving a review on the platform from where you purchased the book. Thank you very much!

I adore hearing from my readers! I can be found on Facebook at https://www.facebook.com/LauraScottBooks, Twitter at https://twitter.com/laurascottbooks, and my website at https://www.laurascottbooks.com. Also, if you sign up for my newsletter, you get a free novella that is not for sale at any vendor. Joining my newsletter will also allow you to hear about the new releases for the rest of the series. Don't miss out, sign up today!

Yours in faith,
    Laura Scott

Naomi Palmer shrank into the corner of the back seat of the car, as far away from the leering man beside her, as she could manage.

She'd thought following the boxy white van would get her a step closer to finding her sixteen-year-old half-sister, Kate, but she hadn't anticipated they'd notice her vehicle behind them and send someone after her. She hadn't been prepared when a car had rear-ended her, sending her spinning out of control.

Since her goal was to find her sister, Naomi had gone along with the leering man without putting up a fight.

A decision she second guessed with every passing second and every passing mile. Especially since the white van had disappeared from view around the curvy mountainous road. The Smoky Mountains outside Chattanooga Tennessee were beautiful, but she sensed the majestic hills held terrible secrets.

Was her sister being held somewhere in the mountains? Or had she already been moved to a new location?

"Where are you taking me?" Naomi tried to keep her

voice steady, but felt her strength slipping beneath waves of fear and panic.

What if she couldn't get away? What if they drugged her, or worse?

*Kate? Where are you? Are you okay? Or am I already too late?*

"You'll find out soon enough." The leering man's guttural voice sent tendrils of dread down her spine. Naomi didn't dare take her eyes from him. The vehicle wasn't going that fast, the curves in the road prevented them from speeding, yet she feared jumping from the car could cause more harm than what these men had planned for her.

A risk she may be forced to take.

*Dear Lord, help me! Guide me! Protect me!*

"Find a place to pull over," the leering man said to the driver. Her pulse spiked as the vehicle slowed, as if it was about to make a turn. A quick glance confirmed there was nothing but a dirt road looming up ahead.

*They were going to rape and kill her.* The thought popped into her head as she understood the magnitude of her foolish actions. It was now or never. As much as she wanted to find Kate, she couldn't let these two men hurt her.

Feeling behind her for the door handle, Naomi took a deep breath, then abruptly lashed out with her foot, catching the unsuspecting leering man beneath his chin with a fierce kick. His head snapped back, hitting the window sharply. At the same moment, she opened the passenger door, and rolled out of the moving car.

Years of gymnastics and cheerleading helped her now. Her teeth snapped together as she hit the pavement hard, but she didn't hesitate. Rolling with the momentum of her fall, she quickly leaped to her feet and sprinted as fast as she could in the opposite direction.

The car behind her stopped and she knew the two men would be hot on her trail. But that didn't worry her as much as being trapped in the car with them.

Naomi headed into the dense woods, using the brush for cover. It was difficult going, but she ignored the scratches from the brambles, her desperate gaze searching for a place to hide.

The two men crashed into the woods behind her. They were large and out of shape, so she felt good about her head start and her ability to lose them. Yet she worried there were more men who could be called in to assist in finding her.

She wouldn't, couldn't let that happen.

Leaping over low bushes and using the larger trees for cover helped create a bigger gap from the men behind her. They were swearing and blaming each other for her escape, which made her smile grimly.

When exhaustion finally overwhelmed her, she dropped behind a large tree and took several deep breaths in an attempt calm her racing heart. She listened intently but didn't hear anything.

Because the men had stopped searching? Or because they'd called in reinforcements and were waiting for them to arrive?

She shivered and took in another deep breath. No sense in borrowing trouble, as her mother would have said. Naomi would have to take the threats one at a time.

Peering around the tree trunk, she searched for any sign of the men. Darkness was falling fast, which was both a blessing and a curse. When she didn't see anything behind her, she decided to keep going, but quietly this time. She desperately wanted more distance between herself and the leering man.

Her t-shirt was torn, her right shoulder and elbow throbbing painfully from where she'd hit the pavement. She wore running shoes which weren't as good over the rough terrain as sturdy hiking boots. Still, Naomi pressed forward, moving silently through the woods.

Estimating the time to be about eight-thirty in the evening, she figured she had barely thirty minutes of daylight yet, maybe less considering her position beneath the thick canopy of trees. Thankfully, the June temperatures were warm. While she wasn't an avid camper, she took some comfort in knowing she wouldn't freeze to death if she had to spend the night in the woods.

Not that there weren't other dangers. Like more men searching for her. Oh, and wild animals. Mountain lions. Bears.

*Gulp.*

Naomi moved in what she hoped was a parallel path to the road. She didn't want to meet up with the leering man and his buddy, but she didn't want to get lost in the forest, either.

Would they expect her to follow the road? Had they gone back to get the car? Were they out on the road, waiting for her to emerge from the brush?

Naomi wasn't sure what to do, other than continue moving through the woods. Time had no meaning, although her surroundings grew darker and darker as the sun dropped behind the horizon. When she stumbled across what looked in the darkness to be an actual hiking trail, she hesitated.

Use the trail? Or stay hidden?

Torn with indecision, she glanced up toward the

dark sky.

*Lord, help me! Guide me!*

A sense of peace draped her like a cloak. She glanced back at the trail, noting it headed down the slope of the mountain in the general direction where she believed the road to be located.

Steeling her resolve, she walked along the path, alert to any hint of someone following. She was surrounded by silence, broken only by the occasional hooting of an owl, or belching tree frog.

She felt alone in this section of the woods.

*For now.*

After another ten minutes of hiking, she abruptly stopped when she caught a glimpse of the black top mountain road between the trees. Her pulse skyrocketed and she dropped down along the edge of the trail, intently watching it.

The vehicle the men had used to rear-end her was an older model black Buick. But in the darkness, she'd never be able to tell if the car going past on the road was a Buick or something else. She swallowed hard. Naomi wasn't sure how long she crouched there, but when her knees protested the position, she slowly rose and continued easing down the trail. No easy task in the darkness that both shielded her and created a treacherous descent.

When she rounded a curve, the road disappeared from sight. She decided leaving the trail was probably best, to stay hidden from view.

But moving through the brush created more noise than she liked. Again, she was torn by indecision. She took one step forward, then another.

The rumbling sound of an engine made her freeze. It was loud, not a car, she quickly deduced, but maybe a truck.

Easing forward to see the stretch of the road better, she watched a pair of high wide headlights along with several smaller yellow lights along the top, roll into view. A semi-truck!

*Wait for me!* Naomi knew her chance to escape this nightmare was driving right past her. She crashed through the brush and ran as fast as she dared down the trail toward the road. But she was too late. By the time she'd gotten halfway there, the truck was no longer in view.

*No!* She bent over, resting her hands on her knees, trying not to cry. She pulled herself together with an effort. Okay, at least she knew this road saw some traffic other than the men in the black Buick who were no doubt still out there, trying to find her.

Naomi continued on the path heading toward the road. Of course, she didn't see any more traffic going by. She told herself to be glad there was no sign of a dark colored sedan. Upon reaching the bottom of the trail she paused by a tree located near the side of the road.

Another vehicle was approaching. Not the loud rumble of a semi-truck trailer, unfortunately.

Tensing with fear, she eased further backward into the brush, just in case the car was the black Buick. But when she caught a glimpse of a pale car, along with the red and white light rack stretched across the top, she leaped forward stumbling out onto the road, waving her arms over her head like a maniac.

"I'm here! I'm here!" Naomi wasn't sure why she was yelling those words, it wasn't as if the cop behind the wheel had been out searching for her. "Help me!"

To her overwhelming relief, the squad pulled over to the side and came to a jarring stop. Tears pricked her eyes as she ran forward.

"Ma'am? Are you all right?" A tall officer with short dark hair, slid out from behind the wheel, eyeing her warily. She noticed he rested his right hand on his gun.

"I-I escaped, two men grabbed me, black Buick—" she stopped realizing she was babbling. "They rear-ended me, then kidnapped me," she finally managed.

"Do you have a weapon?" The cop eyed her warily as he moved forward. Naomi knew she looked like a crazy woman, her blonde hair snarled from the brush and her clothing ripped and torn.

She stared at him blankly, then shook her head. "No."

The name tag beneath his badge identified him as Murphy. He raked his gaze over her. "What about drugs?"

"No!" She was growing impatient now. "I don't have anything, because they kidnapped me!"

"Okay, but I need to be sure, for my safety and yours." Officer Murphy stepped closer, finally dropping his hand from his gun. He quickly patted her jean pockets, then glanced over her shoulder. "You escaped and hid in the woods?"

"Yes." Reaction from her ordeal had set in, and she found herself shivering despite the warm temperatures. "I— think they—were going to r—ape and k-ill me."

Officer Murphy's dark brown eyes filled with compassion. He rested a reassuring hand on her shoulder. "It's okay, you're safe now."

She gave a jerky nod, still shivering uncontrollably. The cop gently guided her to the squad, opening the front passenger door, rather than the rear one, a small gesture she appreciated. "Get inside, I'll keep you safe," he promised.

After sliding into the passenger seat, she rested her head against the cushion and let out a long sigh.

She believed him.

www.ingramcontent.com/pod-product-compliance
Lightning Source LLC
Chambersburg PA
CBHW071258190726

48292CB00007B/2592